DUST OVER WARPATH

DUST OVER WARPATH

by

Erle Russell

Dales Large Print Books
Long Preston, North Yorkshire,
BD23 4ND, England.

British Library Cataloguing in Publication Data.

Russell, Erle
    Dust over Warpath.

      A catalogue record of this book is
      available from the British Library

      ISBN   978-1-84262-882-9 pbk

First published in Great Britain in 1953 by Hennel Locke Ltd.

Copyright © Erle Russell

Cover illustration © Michael Thomas

The moral right of the author has been asserted

Published in Large Print 2012 by arrangement with
Erle Russell, care of Watson, Little Ltd.

Dales Large Print is an imprint of Library Magna Books Ltd.

Printed and bound in Great Britain by
T.J. (International) Ltd., Cornwall, PL28 8RW

FOR
BARBARA STANWYCK
IN APPRECIATION

CONTENTS

Contents

Chapter I

Shelby Comes to Warpath

The silence of the hot June morning, unbroken save for a few small, distant noises, laid itself over the town of Warpath like an invisible garment.

The only sounds which came to the ears of the lone rider coming in from the eastern trail were the faint lifting of voices from the tin Baptist church, the muffled chords of the harmonium and the fast-vanishing rattle of the Express coach as it breasted the ribbon-like trail on its outward trip to the west.

Kent Shelby riding in from the farther side of town had too often heard the crunch of six-foot, iron-bound wheels and the rattle of harness and the clip-clop of a lunging six-horse team to be in any doubt that a stage or Express coach had but recently stopped here on its journey farther westward.

Indeed, the dust had hardly settled on the hot, sticky air as the travel-stained rider lifted his nose like a dog scenting out a smell.

Now the soft sound of voices and music

11

had ceased and Shelby figured the parson was maybe talking to the congregation in a voice that would not carry this far.

Presently a dog barked and a few kids, temporarily released from parental control, raised their voices and indulged in the uninhibited savagery of kids the world over.

Shelby was in no hurry to explore the town as he viewed the first of the clap-board buildings. Warpath, he figured, was just another cow-town, but maybe the valley was good for cattle. He hoped so; otherwise he would be stuck with a ranch that maybe would not pay. A ranch he had never seen and had bought with the last of his money during a wild, drunken jag in Three Forks!

A rueful smile touched his broad-lipped mouth as he speculated on whether the, as yet unseen, Sugar Loaf spread would prove to be an ace or a joker. Neither, possibly; just another card with little or no value against the aces and kings of other of the valley ranchers.

He pushed the low-crowned stetson to the back of his jet-black hair and built a smoke, letting his idle gaze drift ahead and settle and move on like the passage of a tired or undecided buzz-fly.

Once again the soft voices rose from the church, muted by distance and the confining walls of the buildings; and then other sounds, nearer at hand, broke sharply into

12

Shelby's train of thought, over-riding the voices of the worshippers, the distant shouts of kids and even covering for a few moments the yapping of the dog.

Horses had come into town from some direction as yet undiscovered by Shelby. There was an urgent haste about the sharp, quickly halted hoof-beats.

Men's voices were raised for a few moments and then again quiet descended, only to be broken by the sound of a six-gun, its blast roaring and echoing around buildings until it reached the alley-way in which Kent Shelby had halted the sorrel.

He stubbed out the cigarette on the dark, service-stained saddle-horn and his booted feet found stirrups even as the rataplan of racing hooves shook the flimsy buildings with the force of their reverberations.

Gently, almost casually, he pricked the sorrel's flanks with the long-rowelled spurs and brought it out on to the street ahead which he found to be an offshoot of Main.

He raced the horse now, to the end of the street, conscious of one or two figures appearing at windows in half-aroused curiosity.

He sawed on the reins as the sorrel hit Main. It was unexpectedly wide for a small cow-town street and a short distance away it widened still more into something like a town square. Here the little tin church stood, now partly screened by buggies, rigs, a spring-wagon and a few saddle-horses.

All this he saw in a lightning glance before his gaze switched to three riders fast disappearing down a side-street to the left.

He glimpsed the mail sacks across the saddles of the two leading horsemen and took in the black bandannas which half covered the faces of the three riders.

A gun flashed and winked in the sunlight of this Sabbath morning and Shelby felt a kind of bitter satisfaction as his second shot unsaddled the last of the trio as the man all but disappeared from view round the corner.

The two leading riders were gone in a swirl of dust and immediately Shelby saw the futility of attempting to follow them through unknown alley-ways and side-streets which would be, to a stranger, little less than a maze.

Already, he decided, they would be making for the tangled trails of the low hills which at one point almost overhung the clapboard town.

He sheathed the smoking six-gun and put the horse forward to where the lone figure lay, stiff and still, in the bright sunlight. The man's horse had run on with the others. Some time later it might be found, if it did not wander back to its home corral.

Shelby had almost reached the fallen desperado, when people spilled from the church. He saw a sheriff's star glinting in the sunlight, glimpsed the drawn gun and the handlebar moustaches on the sun-burned face, and heard a woman scream: 'There's one of them–!'

The broad back that he turned to the woman as he stooped over the sprawled out-law was in itself a gesture of studied con-tempt. Contempt for such a one, be it man or woman, who could rush thus upon a scene and differentiate innocent and guilty with such supreme confidence and yet lack the clear thinking necessary under these con-ditions.

He heard the sheriff call 'Wait!' and had no way of knowing, and did not care, whether the lawman referred to himself or the woman who had screamed hysterically.

The man at his feet was dead and Kent could see where the second bullet had gone into his back, shattering the spine and spilling the young robber's lifeblood.

He straightened up then, after tearing the black bandanna from the set, mask-like face, and Sheriff Tom Borden said, 'That's George – "Curly" – Armstrong, folks. Looks like the stranger's rid us of one road-agent we been looking for.'

The girl spoke for the second time, glancing sharply towards Shelby.

'You mean he's not–?'

Shelby smiled but there was no humour in

15

his eyes.

'You believe in shooting first and asking questions when it's too late, ma'am?'

An elderly woman, dressed in black, muttered, 'It's disgraceful,' and her spouse nodded approvingly and followed her away from the crowd.

A lean, middle-aged man, wearing a deputy's badge, thrust forward to join the sheriff.

'What happened, mister?' he said laying his stone-like gaze on Shelby's face. 'How come you were around?'

'There was another shot before this one,' Shelby explained. 'I heard it as I was entering town. Came from over there, I reckon.'

'My Gawd!' the deputy said. 'The Wells-Fargo office! The miners' pay-roll came in a half-hour back!'

The sheriff's eyes turned on the woman who had screamed and Shelby sensed something here that he did not quite understand. It was almost as though she had expected something like this to happen. Now she murmured the one name, 'Johnnie,' softly, and Tom Borden gestured to his deputy.

'Look after Miss Montago, Vern, while I go down to the office. Brad! Henry!' he called, 'you two are deppities. Look after things!' He swung his glance at Shelby as he spoke and turned and walked down the hot, dusty street towards the Wells-Fargo office half-

16

way through the town.

Isobel Montago said in a voice strangely flat. 'I must go, Vern, let me go and see—'

'You stay right here, Miss Montago,' Vern Hanson drawled; but the girl wrenched herself free of his restraining hand and, unmindful of the crowd, picked up her trailing skirts and ran in the direction taken by the sheriff.

Hanson said, 'She asked fer it!'

Now some of the congregation broke away, a few making for their waiting buggies and rigs. There were still two-score or more people when Sheriff Tom Borden came back, supporting the half-fainting girl.

'Johnnie's bin killed,' Borden told them, 'and the miners' pay-roll swiped.'

A girl spoke from the outskirts of the crowd and Kent Shelby's gaze lifted at her voice. There was a flair of interest in his face as he watched her drop the reins of the horse she had been leading and step through the lane formed for her by the milling townsfolk.

'I'll see Miss Montago home, sheriff,' she said in a low, throaty voice, and Borden's wooden face relaxed enough to show gratitude.

'Thanks, Miss Hale. Reckon she needs someone to look after her. Gill! Better roust out Doc Cleary—'

'I'm here,' a voice said as a smallish, rather portly man pushed forward. 'I'll go along

17

with 'em both.'

Now the girl addressed as Miss Hale could see the sprawled figure of the desperado and her green eyes slid to Shelby's face. She took in the scene with a detached calm which Kent Shelby found himself admiring.

'You killed him?' she said. It was more of a statement than a question and Shelby inclined his head, taking in the breathless beauty of this girl with her green eyes and black hair underneath the pushed-back stetson. The wide, red mouth moved in a half-smile of acknowledgement as she turned and placed a strong arm around Isobel Montago's waist.

On the other side Doc Cleary gave his support and together they helped the half-conscious girl towards the schoolhouse just visible beyond the square.

'Now,' Tom Borden said. 'We haven't time to waste. You, Gil, Brad, Henry, Jack, get your horses. We'll be heading out after those killers in a minute.'

He turned to a man dressed in Sunday black. 'Jim! Get some help and take the body down to the office. I'll want to look at it later.' His glance came back to Shelby.

'Well, stranger, tell us your name and what happened and make it fast!'

Kent began to build a cigarette.

'The name's Kent Shelby,' he said, 'and I was coming into town from over there.' He

18

pointed to the side-street up which he had raced the sorrel. 'At the bottom of the street I was,' he went on, 'in an alley, smoking a cigarette. Guess the stub's still there where I threw it,' he smiled.

Borden nodded impatiently. 'Go on.'

'Heard what I took to be the stage or Express coach pulling out to the west. Heard the congregation singing and then the sound of horses coming in fast.'

'Then what?' Borden said.

'Guess nothing for a few minutes. Then a single shot. I figured it was time to take a look. I brought the sorrel up from the alley into that side-street and hit Main just in time to see three masked riders.'

'What did they look like?'

Shelby smiled and shook his head.

'All I could see was that the first two seemed to have gunny-sacks across their saddles in front and that the men had black bandannas. Beyond that–' He shrugged. 'Ordinary range rig, I guess. I only had a few seconds to draw a bead on the third one bringing up the rear. My second shot got him, as you can see.'

Tom Borden nodded. 'You'd better come with us, Shelby. Afterwards I'll want you in case there are any more questions.'

Kent nodded and indicated the dust-caked sorrel. 'My horse is tired and in need of water and feed–'

Borden said, 'We'll fix you with a mount. Here come the men now. Vern! Get Shelby a horse from the livery!'

The sheriff, deputy Vern Hanson, and special deputies Brad Straw and Henry Guyler led the small posse from town, following the tracks of the robbers' horses, still visible in the dust of Warpath.

Kent Shelby found himself riding with Jack Summers of the blacksmith's shop. He was a quiet man and for this Shelby was grateful. He had his own thoughts as company and looked upon the episode of the posse taking out into the badlands as a probable waste of time; although, obviously, Sheriff Tom Borden had a job to do and such a chore as this was part of it, however seemingly futile it might appear to an outsider.

As they moved slowly out of town, figuring out the direction taken by the two road-agents, Shelby thought back on the events that had led up to his arrival in Warpath.

He even allowed himself a thin-lipped smile as he recollected the way Kate Trafford had two-timed him, leading him along like a dumb dogie to the slaughter, only to laugh in his face and up and marry the dashing Sid Schuler. That was in Silverbell.

Shelby had then saddled up the sorrel, packed his warbag and drawn all his savings from the small 'dobe bank. He had wanted more than anything at that moment to shake the dust of Silverbell from his feet and put distance as well as time between himself and the blue-eyed, golden-haired girl whose image still haunted him, so that the pain in his belly was a steady, dull ache.

At Three Forks he had met up with Charlie Colfax and Cal Eddy, two rangy oldsters who had ridden the chucklines with him in Texas and New Mexico territory.

Shelby's habitually cold, aloof reserve gradually slipped from him as the liquor flowed and then Gus Garner, somehow or other, had joined the party, in search of whisky and money.

Kent grinned again as he thought back on the drunkenly voiced protestations as he had tried to give Gus Garner all the money he had. Even then Shelby had not been so far gone that he was unable to recollect a good deal of what had taken place.

Gus Garner had gravely insisted that Shelby should have something for the money he was offering.

'I cain't take twen'y thousand dollars off'n you, mister, not without givin' yuh somethin' back in return,' Garner had insisted with the studied seriousness of a man whose speech was already beginning to slur.

'Fair enough,' Charlie Colfax had hiccupped, wiping the bedraggled long-horn moustaches with the cuff of his shirt-sleeve.

'You give him the money, Kent,' he said, 'an' Gus'll give you– What you goin' to offer, Gus?'

Garner then withdrew a sheaf of legal-looking documents together with a bill of sale for his stock and managed to sign the papers more or less in the right places. Shelby too, with a great effort of concentration and considerable help from Cal Eddy and Charlie Colfax, managed to affix a shaky signature somewhere on the title deeds.

Quite content now, Gus Garner quit the party and Shelby stuffed the papers away in his shirt and proceeded to make a night of it.

Later, much later, Kent Shelby had awakened to find himself the owner of a ranch he had never seen and never even heard of. Sugar Loaf was the brand and it was situated in a valley, the nearest town to which was a place called Warpath.

The following afternoon Kent made the rounds of Three Forks until he had found Colfax and Eddy, to whom he explained the situation.

After a wash-up and a meal, the two stringy oldsters had felt more capable of reviewing the situation and there and then Shelby had taken them on as cow-hands.

'You two go ahead and take over,' Shelby had told them. 'I've found out Warpath is thirty miles west from here along the stage trail. Get on to Sugar Loaf and throw off any trespassers. I'll join you in a day or two!'

They had saddled up and had ridden off with the natural unconcern of their kind, content to wait for Shelby whether he took a day or a month or a year.

Nevertheless, that had been three days ago. Shelby had hit the bottle again in Mesquite Flats in a final effort to drown the memory of a blue-eyed girl.

Now he was feeling impatient to get to the spread. So far he had not mentioned his connection with Sugar Loaf nor even asked its whereabouts.

Ahead of him the leaders had stopped for a consultation and when Jack Summers and Shelby rode up they found the posse had come to a full-stop.

'Reckon the tracks 've petered out on this shale,' Borden told them. 'It's anybody's guess which way they went from here.'

It had been noon, almost, when they had set off. Now the westering sun showed the time as being somewhere near four o'clock.

Borden pulled a silver timepiece from his calf-skin vest, casting an oblique glance at the sun as though to confirm that the heavenly firmament was still functioning correctly.

'Just after four, men. Guess we've bin ridin' too long already. My belly's wanting its dinner!'

Several voices agreed with the sheriff's sentiments and with a last glance at the rocky country ahead, Borden swung his mount round, pointing it towards the distant town.

The horses too sensed food and, tired as they were, they exerted themselves so that the posse entered town in a little over an hour and a half's steady riding.

A late Sunday dinner was better than no dinner at all; the men grinned as they beat dust from their clothes and led horses back to barn and corral.

Shelby followed Borden and Vern Hanson into the office and waited whilst the sheriff went through the dead Curly Armstrong's clothes.

He laid the man's possessions on his desk and gave instructions to Vern to have the body removed to Shilo Cleburne's funeral parlour.

'Now, Shelby,' Tom Borden said, pouring himself a drink and pushing one across the desk for Kent, 'we didn't have much time for details before, I reckon. Let's have the full story!'

Chapter II

Sugar Loaf

After Doc Cleary had left the schoolhouse, Donna Hale busied herself with preparing a light meal for herself and Isobel.

She carried a tray into the parlour from the kitchen and set it down on a small table near the sofa on which Isobel Montago lay.

Donna pulled up a straight-backed chair and her green eyes slid to the girl who had so lately lost her brother.

'You must try and eat something, Isobel,' Donna said presently. 'At least drink some coffee, it will do you good. Talk if you want to, my dear. Perhaps it will help. What about school tomorrow? Don't you think you ought to go away some place for a vacation?'

'You are kind, Donna,' Isobel said, blinking back the tears that threatened to start afresh.

She shook her head slowly and Donna admired the red, dancing lights reflected in her hair from the sunlight coming in at the window.

'I think it will be better if I carry right on with teaching the children,' Isobel said.

'They need me and it might take a long time to fill my place even for a short period.'

Suddenly she began talking about her brother, and Donna listened, understanding the relief the other girl found in talking about her Johnnie.

'He was all set to buy Sugar Loaf, Donna, did you know? Johnnie has always been crazy on cattle. Why, for years he has saved from what he earned working in the Wells-Fargo office. Then when Dad died there was a little for each of us. Not a great deal, but it helped. It meant that after hard saving for ten years, Johnnie could just about buy Sugar Loaf if Gus Garner didn't want too much for it.'

'But I don't understand, Isobel. My own father has tried to buy Sugar Loaf from Garner several times. Each time Gus refused. Said he wasn't figuring on selling anyway.'

Isobel Montago shrugged the mild objection aside. Her own grief was still too young and too heavy to allow room for other folks' troubles at the moment.

Her jarred mind flew off at a tangent. 'Johnnie should never have been left on his own in that office,' she said. 'Borden or Hanson should have been along, particularly as the Wells-Fargo coach was bringing the miners' pay. And what about the stranger who supposedly shot one of the murderers, Donna? How do we know he wasn't one of them?'

Donna Hale shook her head gently and the wide, red mouth parted in a smile. 'He killed one of the outlaws, Isobel,' she reminded the schoolteacher, 'and besides, he's not a killer–'

'How could you possibly know that, Donna? You've only seen him the once. Why we don't even know his name, where he comes from, who he is, or anything!'

'Some things you just know, Isobel, particularly about a man like that!'

It was dark when Donna Hale left the schoolhouse and walked towards the town livery for her horse. She did not much relish the seven-mile ride at night along the floor of the valley to the Horseshoe spread but – well, she had done it before – and Isobel had needed comfort and companionship, particularly on this day.

She would see the sheriff and Shilo Cleburne and fix things for Isobel with regard to Johnnie's funeral. This much at least she could do.

Shelby downed the proffered whisky and lit a cigarette whilst Borden lit the lamps.

'Who was the girl who figured me as being one of the killers, sheriff?'

Borden lit the last map and dropped the chimney back in place before he spoke.

'That's Isobel Montago, the schoolteacher.

It was her brother Johnnie who took the slug apparently trying to stop them bustards from lifting the miners' pay. But you answer my questions fust, Shelby. Fill in the gaps you left. Better start right from the beginning!'

Kent grinned and fished the title deeds of Sugar Loaf from his pocket and threw them on the desk, together with his bill of sale, for the sheriff's perusal.

'Perhaps this is as good a place as any to start,' he suggested. 'Back in Three Forks I met up with two old saddle-pards of mine. Charlie Colfax and Cal Eddy. We were drinking. Next we knew, this Gus Garner decides to set in. Says he wants *dinero*. Guess we didn't bother to ask why. Wasn't our business and in any case we were getting a mite drunk–'

Sheriff Tom Borden's glance moved over Shelby's face. He was intensely interested.

'Go on, Shelby.'

Kent said. 'I had my life savings on me. I was getting to hell out of Silverbell on account of a woman two-timed me. That don't matter, but that's how it was I had left town and had over twen'y thousand dollars with me. Garner gave me these deeds and I gave him my money. I guess we were both too high to know much what we were doing, but Colfax and Eddy witnessed it.

'Next morning I realized I'd bought a ranch I'd never seen or even heard of. I fixed with

Colfax and Eddy to go on ahaid and come to Warpath, then light out for Sugar Loaf. Told them I'd follow in a day or two. Guess I kept on thinking of the girl in Silverbell and when I reached Mesquite Flats I drowned this woman for the second time in rye whiskey.' The smile touched Shelby's flat-planed face but lightly. 'Reckon I slept most of Saturday and came on to Warpath next morning. You know what happened after that.'

There was a long silence broken only by the ticking of the cheap clock on the wall.

Cigarette smoke wreathed itself round the oil lamps. Finally Borden refilled the two empty glasses.

'It's a good job for you you've got witnesses, Shelby. If you have! I was notified Friday night that Gus Garner's body had been dragged outa Rock Creek. The marshal of Silverbell is handling it and as Gus Garner had no kith or kin it don't matter much where he's buried.'

Tom Borden thought for a moment, before continuing, sizing this man Kent Shelby and finally coming to a decision.

'Heard tell that Mason Hale had been after Gus for some long time to buy Sugar Loaf but Gus didn't seem keen to sell. Seems strange when you think of it, Shelby, that he went to Three Forks, got drunk and then sold stock and ranch to a complete stranger – you!'

'I'll admit it does seem queer,' Shelby replied, drawing smoke into his lungs and expelling twin streamers from his nostrils. 'But you can check up on this signature, can't you?' he asked, indicating Gus Garner's sprawled name on the papers. 'Maybe he was as near drunk as I was but I guess that's more or less his normal scrawl.'

Borden nodded. 'There'll be papers at Sugar Loaf no doubt, if you don't mind me having a look-see, sometime. Meanwhile I kinda recollect I've got a note of Gus's somewhere around in my desk. That would do well enough to check the writing.'

Tom Borden paused again and his glance was bright in the lamplight as he looked up from underneath craggy brows.

'I guess your story ties in, Shelby,' he said. 'Marshal Fayette of Silverbell included the information that there was near to twen'y thousand dollars on Garner after he'd been fished out of the creek. That makes it look more like a genuine accident than anyone pushed him in.'

'Could be that he'd gotten so drunk that even the creek didn't sober him,' Kent said.

Tom Borden nodded tiredly. 'I guess I'm goin' home to eat an' sleep, Shelby. It's been a kinda tirin' day. What you figger on doin'?'

'I'll have a meal in town, a drink mebbe, and get along to Sugar Loaf. My boys'll be wondering what's happened.'

Borden stood up and turned down the lights, blowing them out one by one. He followed Kent out into the night where lights spilled their rectangles of bright yellow on to the plank-walk and dusty street.

'Your sorrel's at Gil's feed barn, yonder,' the sheriff said pointing down the street with his arm. 'I'm goin' to fix with the coroner to hold the inquest on Curly Armstrong and Johnnie tomorrow, ten o'clock sharp, in the school hall. That's separate from the school-house,' the sheriff explained intercepting Shelby's glance. 'Won't interfere with Miss Montago. You'll be there?'

Kent nodded and the sheriff strode away, his 'goodnight' washed away by the slowly building crescendo of sound as Warpath got under way for the night.

She stood flat against the clap-board wall outside the feed barn and near to the dimly lit entrance, watching him.

He stopped suddenly, one foot on the bottom step of the board-walk, as he felt the impact of her gaze pushing into him and realized that she stood thus and had watched him from the time he had left the sheriff's office.

The hurricane lamp hanging at the entrance to Gil's livery painted the nearer half of her face and body in a warm yellow. The left side of her, from stetson-crowned head

31

to spurred feet, was a dark, bluish silhouette.

He came up the steps then, slowly, and said, 'Good evening, Miss Hale,' and commenced building himself a cigarette because he found the sight of her, as well as the faint suggestion of perfume, vaguely disturbing.

She continued to gaze at him with her level green eyes and now, nearer to her, he took in the stirring beauty of the dark skin, the swelling breasts underneath the silk shirt, the lissom figure in its divided riding skirt that fell an inch or two short of the boot tops.

'You know my name,' she said in the low, husky voice that he had first heard that same morning. 'They tell me you're called Shelby?'

'They?'

She moved her head slightly, indicating the town generally in a gesture which seemed to say 'It doesn't matter.'

'Kent Shelby,' the man said and smiled as he struck a sulphur match to the cigarette in his mouth.

Now it was the girl's turn to study the face before her, sharply illuminated by the match held in the strong, sunburnt, cupped hands. She saw the thick brows as black or blacker than her own, the grey eyes that could, she knew, come alight at the right times and remain as cold as stones meanwhile. She saw the almost Indian flatness of his face, sharpened rather than softened by the glow from the lighted match. Then he had blown out the light and dimly she watched the spiral of blue smoke ascend and the sharp tang of tobacco smoke came at her nostrils so that they widened to receive the stinging yet pleasurable scent.

He turned and indicated the paint pony tied to the hitchrail a few feet away, noticing even in the immediate gloom the faint Horseshoe H brand on the rump.

'Yours?'

She nodded. 'My father is Mason Hale. We run the Horseshoe H seven miles down the valley.'

'You riding back, tonight, alone?'

She wondered whether there was a hint of concern in his voice or whether it lay only in her own imagination. The man was just being polite.

Now she allowed herself that slight half-smile, similar to the one with which she had acknowledged him this morning.

If before, he thought, she had been like a lovely but perhaps dangerous orchid, she was now, with that smile, a less exotic flower. A flower of the lush river bottoms rather than the hard and vivid-painted blooms of the desert.

'What are you thinking?' she said showing a glint of white teeth.

33

'I was thinking of desert and prairie flowers,' he smiled and observed the faint tinge of colour that over-rode the dark shading on her cheeks.

'You haven't answered my question,' Shelby reminded her. 'If you figure on riding back tonight I would like to ride with you.'

She hesitated for a brief moment and pushed herself gently away from the wall.

'That would be nice, Mr Shelby. I'll wait while you saddle your horse.'

He dropped the cigarette end, grinding it under the toe of his boot and strode easily into the barn. In a matter of seconds he returned, leading the sorrel bridled and saddled. Donna Hale was already aboard and now she led the way by the distance of half a horse until they were clear of town and riding the floor of the valley.

'I heard also, back there, that you are the new owner of Sugar Loaf.'

'Correct,' Kent Shelby said, 'but as far as I can remember I've only mentioned it to the sheriff.'

'Walls have ears.' Donna Hale smiled. 'I guess that's been said a good many times before, but you must know what a small cowtown's like?'

He nodded in the darkness. 'I've known a few.'

'A few thousand, I would say!'

'Why?'

She shrugged. 'You've got the stamp of a man who likes to keep on going–'

'Fiddle-footed, huh?'

She laughed and Shelby thought that the sound held a quality in harmony with her physical beauty.

'It's all the more strange though,' she reflected, 'considering Dad tried to get Gus to sell for months, and failed. Now you, a complete stranger, come over the horizon and calmly state you are the owner of Sugar Loaf! What's happened to Gus. We haven't seen him around for some days. Is he at the ranch?'

Shelby flashed her a quick glance and when it met her level gaze he felt ashamed and irritated at his dawning suspicions.

'Gus is dead, Donna,' Shelby said and wondered at himself.

She reined the paint in sharply and in so doing her body came against Shelby's as the two horses clashed. He caught her hand to steady her and tried hard to conjure up the image of Kate Trafford in his mind's eye. But Kate had green eyes now and black hair instead of yellow. Mentally he shook himself and answered the girl's questions.

'Tom Borden told me. He didn't say to keep it secret, so I guess there's no harm done. He was notified by the marshal of Silverbell that Gus Garner had been fished out of Rock Creek.'

'How horrible,' Donna whispered. 'Poor Gus! He could be ornery at times, but I liked him.'

Shelby saw that the black lashes sparkled with unshed tears. Here was a woman, he thought, who was as forthright as she was lovely and not afraid to wear her heart on her sleeve. They rode steadily on in a silence of mutual sympathy, until the girl reined in the pony again and pointed to a distant scattering of lights.

'Horseshoe,' she said and smiled and held out her hand.

'Thank you, Kent, for riding with me.' She released her hand from his hard grip and pointed south-west. 'You can get to Sugar Loaf across our land now, Kent. From here it's not more than three-four miles.'

He glanced up at the Big Dipper and oriented himself.

'You keep straight on,' she explained, 'and pass between those two distant buttes. See?'

He put his gaze to the indigo-painted country ahead and dimly discerned the twin sentinels to which she referred.

'I couldn't miss it, could I?' He pulled up suddenly as a thought struck him.

'I haven't asked you how Miss Montago is, Donna—?'

She looked at him through the darkness. 'It was nice of you to ask now, Kent. She'll be all right, after a little while, I think. She has the school. She loves children.'

Shelby said, 'I must go and see her sometime. Tomorrow Borden's fixing for the inquest on Johnnie and the outlaw.' Shelby hesitated. 'I'd like for you to come over to Sugar Loaf sometime, Donna, when you're at a loose end–'

'I'd love to, Kent. I don't know whether I'll be able to return the compliment. Dad doesn't take kindly to fresh people and when he hears you've beaten him to it over the ranch–'

Shelby was yet a mile from the black silhouette which he took to be the Sugar Loaf ranch-house when he remembered that he had not partaken of the meal which he had promised himself back in Warpath. Or the drink for that matter. The girl had been standing there almost as though waiting at a trysting place – but that was a dam'-fool, crazy sort of notion...

The bullet came at him out of the night, screaming past like a savage hornet a brief moment after the crack of a carbine. He had glimpsed the muzzle-flash as a tiny island of flame in the surrounding sea of the veranda's darkness. Now, gun in hand, he sat the sorrel, hesitant to send lead flying into his own ranch-house.

'Sing out, dam' yore eyes!' a voice snarled

37

from the darkness of the house and the tension came out of Kent Shelby slowly as he recognized the brittle voice of Cal Eddy.

'Shelby here,' Kent sang out. 'Put that dam' cannon up, Cal!'

A grunt came out of the shadows ahead and then boots echoed on wooden steps and crunched on the gravel of the yard.

Shelby swung out of leather as Eddy came up, a carbine in the crook of his arm.

'What's wrong, Cal?' Kent asked the question as he threw the reins over the sorrel's head and withdrew his own carbine from the saddle-boot.

'We's had visitors earlier on, Kent,' Eddy rasped. 'Figgered you was one of 'em returnin', mebbe. They shot up the ranch some. Broke most o' the windows. A stray slug caught Charlie, though he ain't bad hurt. Come inside. I'll put yore hoss up later.'

Shelby followed Cal up the veranda steps, through the screen door into a small square hall. To the right a lamp glowed dully from the half-open door of the living-room.

Inside, Cal turned up the lamp, and Kent had a sudden quick view of gunny-sacks hanging over partly shattered windows before his gaze swung round to Colfax lying back on the deep sofa, a bandage around his black-grey head.

There were splinters of wood and slivers

of glass which Cal had swept into a neat pile in the hearth, in which logs burned, giving a warmth and cheerfulness to the room in spite of everything.

Colfax's black eyes were on Shelby and the oldster's long-horn moustache twitched. Kent knew he was grinning.

'Ain't more'n a scratch, Kent,' he said, 'but you know what Eddy is. Kinda figgered I was bleedin' to death, I reckon, the way he jumped about an' insisted on bandagin' me up.'

Shelby sank into a leather chair and commenced rolling a cigarette. He threw sack and papers across to Charlie.

Cal said, 'Mebbe you could use some cawfee?'

Shelby nodded. 'And anything that's going, to eat, Cal.'

Eddy nodded and tramped out to the kitchen.

Colfax reached down to the floor beside him, lifting a fair-sized stone on which was tied a piece of paper.

Shelby leaned forward and took the stone, reading the crudely scrawled pencil message.

GET OFF SUGAR LOAF WHILE THE GOIN'S GOOD. NEXT TIME YOU MIGHT GET HURT.

Charlie said, 'Thet came through the window this mawnin'. Cal figgered he heerd riders comin'. By the time he was out front they'd come into the yard–'

'Know who they were, Charlie?' Colfax said. 'I didn't see 'em close like Cal did. He figgered they was wearin' a Horseshoe H brand.'

'Ah,' Shelby breathed and sent cigarette smoke down his nostrils.

'Better let Cal tell the rest, 'cos jest after they throwed thet rock they started slingin' lead. Our belts was on our bunks with our carbines, so we had to duck down on the floor. Soon after a bullet creased me an' knocked me cold.'

Eddy came in bearing a tin plate of thickly cut meat sandwiches. Shelby started in on them, feeling the slight hunger pains in his empty belly.

Cal poured three cups of coffee from a battered tin pot and rolled himself a smoke. He had heard the conversation from the kitchen and now filled in the gaps while Kent ate his food.

'Five riders there was, Kent,' Cal said, 'ridin' Horseshoe H ponies. The ramrod was a tough, salty *hombre*. Said he wanted to see the boss. I acted kinda dumb–'

'You didn't hevta act,' Colfax grunted.

Eddy ignored the interruption. 'Like he said, they chucked thet rock in through the window an' started shootin' up the place a bit. I came in then an' we ducked down on the floor. Charlie was hit an' I crawled back to the bedroom fer our guns. Time I was back I heard their hosses beatin' a retreat. Time I got out on the veranda they were sure hittin' the dust. I sent a coupla slugs after 'em, but I don't figger I hit anythin'.'

Shelby pushed the empty plate across the pinewood table, reached for the coffee-cup.

'It looks like the familiar story of the big man trying to push the small one out,' Kent said. 'Now I'll tell you my side of the story and then you'll probably figure same as I do. We've got a fight on our hands with Horseshoe H if we stay here. If we don't want a fight we can sell the ranch to Mason Hale who owns Horseshoe and pack our warbags and ride on–'

'Who said anythin' about ridin' on, Kent?' Cal demanded.

Charlie pointed to his bandaged head. His black eyes glinted fiercely. 'You don't figger I'm takin' this lyin' down, do you?'

Chapter III

Chip Bander's Ultimatum

In spite of the comparatively late session the previous night, Sugar Loaf was astir bright and early Monday morning. Shelby was anxious to have a quick look over the buildings in the first light of day, to inspect the land in the immediate vicinity of the ranchhouse before setting out for the inquest at Warpath.

Like the old campaigners they were, Cal and Charlie had not been idle since hitting Sugar Loaf. In the light from coal-oil lamps at early breakfast, Shelby had inspected the canned goods which the two hands had bought at Warpath, without, however, disclosing their connection with Sugar Loaf. In the absence of specific instructions from Shelby they had played their hand quietly; had learned the whereabouts of Sugar Loaf without actually asking direct questions. Thus, to Warpath, they had been merely a couple of line-riding cow-hands, who had come into town and had departed almost immediately with scarcely a ripple.

Now as the sun rose and drew the valley

mists upwards, Cal and Eddy followed Shelby outside, indicating the out-buildings, the pole corral, the stables and barns. There was even a small blacksmith's shop, though everywhere the grey, cobwebby hand of neglect was apparent.

'Ain't nuthin' here thet cain't be put right with a few nails an' timber an' a few pots of paint,' Colfax grunted.

'I shoved the sorrel in along with our hosses last night, Kent,' Eddy said. 'Found three cow-ponies here in the next barn. Reckon this Gus Garner musta had a coupla hands one time.'

Shelby nodded thoughtfully.

'I still cain't figure why Garner should sell to me when Horseshoe had been after this place so long. Moreover, I don't doubt Horseshoe would have offered more than I could pay. Why?'

Cal scratched his head. 'Heerd in town thar's copper mines a few miles north– Wait a minute! Am I still drunk or did Gus Garner say somethin' about copper bein' on this land?'

Shelby glanced up sharply, frowning, searching the recesses of his mind, going back to the night when the three of them had met up with Gus Garner at Three Forks.

'That seems to strike a chord, Cal,' he said. 'Guess I'd clean forgotten about it the next day but now I'm thinking Garner said he'd hinted to Horseshoe that there were big copper deposits on this land. What we don't know is whether Garner was stringing Hale along for some reason or whether it's really a fact.'

'Supposin' it's true, Kent,' Colfax rasped. 'What d'you figger on doin'?'

Shelby rolled and lit a cigarette before replying. His gaze swept over the rangeland, noting a few distant cattle dotted on the farther slopes.

'I'm a cattle-man first and foremost. If this is good cattle range, if we decide to stick, we'll hold what is ours whether the land is chock full of copper, gold or oil or what else!'

Colfax spat. 'Me too.'

Cal Eddy said, 'If you say the word, Kent, they won't set up no minin' camps on Sugar Loaf!'

Shelby put his gaze to the northern horizon where a dust cloud moved lazily in the brightening morning.

'Riders coming, boys. Better plant yourselves around the house but don't start any shooting. Just be ready.'

Shelby returned to the ranch-house and came out buckling on his gun-belt. Cal and Charlie were nowhere to be seen but Kent knew that at some strategic spot a couple of carbines were there ready to back his play.

The riders were visible now, coming across

Sugar Loaf land, Shelby figured, from the direction of Horseshoe. They were coming in on the same route he himself had used the previous night, straight between the twin buttes a few miles to the north.

Shelby leaned against the veranda rail and waited.

They made no bones about it. There was no attempt to come up quietly. Hooves echoed on the ground, bridles jingled, and men's voices lifted as though their owners' spirits were rising with the sun.

In a surprisingly short space of time they had clattered into the yard and Shelby's cold gaze slanted upwards to the rider who bore the obvious traces of being Horseshoe's ramrod.

The man was big, as big as Shelby, and, unlike the four other riders on their cowponies, sat a tall bay with a blaze forehead.

'Looks like the new boss of Sugar Loaf's come home at last,' a rider said and men laughed as though there were a subtle humour in the words whose meaning and significance they alone shared.

Even Chip Bander, the ramrod, allowed his slit-like mouth to split open and the pale, slate-coloured eyes held a near approach to warmth.

Shelby said evenly. 'I wouldn't start in on breaking any more windows if I were you.'

Chip Bander's grin widened, yet paradoxically the hint of amusement washed out of his eyes, leaving them like cold, wet grey stones.

'Why not, mister? Horseshoe can allus back its own play!'

'There are five of you now, alive,' Shelby said softly. 'Start something and at least three of you won't ever make it back to Horseshoe.'

Bander's gaze slid around Shelby and for the first time he lost a little of his brash confidence. He glanced quickly at the house with the bullet-shattered windows, partly covered by gunny-sacks. One of the sacks moved slightly. Perhaps it was the gentle wind blowing across the valley. Perhaps there was a man behind the window with a carbine trained on them.

Kent leaned back against the rail, his right hand dangling over the butt of his six-gun. There was a relaxed ease about the man that was not entirely lost on Chip Bander and his crew. Bander's hands were in full view on the saddle-horn.

'Listen, mister,' Bander said and his mouth was a mean, ugly line. 'Horseshoe bid fer this spread before you came into the picture. If Gus Garner hadn't gone and drowned hisself, we'd–'

'How did you know Garner had been drowned?' Shelby's question flew out like a snaking bull-whip.

'Why, everyone knows–' Chip Bander said and then he cursed under his breath. He caught himself up quickly as his head thrust forward from the powerful shoulders and his words snarled out of the slit-like mouth.

'We're givin' you twen'y-four hours to get off Sugar Loaf,' he gritted, 'an' we're ready to pay the same price we offered Garner, eighteen thousand. For everythin'. You fix it up with Mason Hale an' everythin'll be jest dandy.'

Shelby grinned. 'All right. You tell me the alternative, *hombre.*'

Bander checked the sudden urge to go for his gun. The subtle emphasis on the word *hombre* had been a calculated insult and Chip had felt the sting just as surely as though he had been at the receiving end of a whip.

He spoke slowly, deliberately and spat the words out with a fierce venom.

'Just three forty-four slugs, mister. That's all, not fired at glazed windows but into the guts of you an' yore sidekicks–'

'Take et easy, Chip, thar's a gun bein' held on yuh from the house!'

Chip Bander breathed hard and his gaze flickered from Shelby's face to the window behind.

'What about Sheriff Borden and the law in Warpath?' Shelby said mildly. 'I hear the town's even got a judge?'

47

The Horseshoe riders guffawed at Shelby's questions and Chip's cold gaze shuttled back to Kent's dark face. He started to say something and then changed his mind.

Finally he spoke again, a flat finality in his voice. 'I wouldn't rely on any law around here, if I was you, mister. Horseshoe's allus gotten what it's gone out for, so far. We don't figger things is changed on account of Sugar Loaf's got a new owner!'

Chip Bander gathered up the bay's reins and shot Kent Shelby a parting warning.

'Twen'y-four hours, mister an' you kin leave in one piece with eighteen thousand dollars. Mebbe the boss would even go to twen'y if you asked him polite!'

With that, Bander swung the horse around and the four riders backed to allow him room to ride forward. Then they put their ponies to a trot, following the ramrod out of the yard.

A couple of the men turned and grinned derisively at Shelby who had not moved from the veranda rail.

In a little while the riders were small moving blobs on the crest of a distant wash towards the twin buttes and Eddy and Colfax joined Kent Shelby, carbines in their hands, gazing after the vanishing Horseshoe riders with a fine contempt.

Shelby rolled a cigarette and leaned against

the school hall wall, watching the townsfolk leave.

The inquest had not taken long. Johnnie Montago had been killed by a shot from one of the three robbers who had stolen the miners' pay from the Wells-Fargo office. George Curly Armstrong had been killed by a shot fired by one, Kent Shelby, the new owner of Sugar Loaf.

The coroner had praised Shelby warmly for his public-spirited action, his quick-thinking and his disregard of personal danger and Kent had noticed Vern Hanson's lip curl.

Horseshoe had been absent and Shelby found himself speculating on Mason Hale, the big noise. His thoughts travelled to Donna as he struggled to unravel the tangled skein of intrigue and mystery which surrounded the whole affair.

He began checking things off in his mind in a systematic way. First Gus Garner had been willing to sell to a stranger rather than let Horseshoe have his ranch and land. But why didn't he just remain there himself and refuse to sell?

There could only be one answer to that, Shelby considered, and that was that Gus Garner was scared and wanted to get out.

'Get out while the goin's good,' Horseshoe had told Shelby. Maybe they had said the same thing to Gus Garner.

But Garner, from what Donna Hale had

said, was an ornery oldster. Maybe he had tried to thwart Mason Hale's scheme by selling to Kent Shelby secretly. Perhaps the old man had hoped to get out of the valley and start somewhere else. But he had finished up at the bottom of Rock Creek.

Shelby stiffened as a new thought was born. If, somehow, Horseshoe had suspected Garner of carrying the title deeds on him, had perhaps even trailed him to Three Forks, might they not have met up with him and knocked him cold, searched him for the deeds and then, drawing a blank, pushed him in the creek, so that his death would appear to have been a drunken misadventure?

It was a startling thought, although Shelby admitted it was mostly guesswork.

Then how did Johnnie Montago set in on this?

Isobel, his sister, had said that Johnnie, too, was in the market for Sugar Loaf, was virtually all set to buy it.

Was there any connection between the death of Garner and Johnnie Montago, or was Johnnie's death something entirely unconnected with other things? Perhaps it had been merely the work of three road-agents out to rob, but supposing there was a connection between the wanted men and Horseshoe?

Kent shook his head and smiled to himself. He was letting his imagination get out of hand!

A bell rang near by and Shelby realized that time had travelled quickly. He heard the kids shouting as they came out of school and guessed that it was noon.

He walked over to the school-house and watched Isobel Montago cross the grassy patch of ground from the school itself.

She was pale, Shelby thought, and he noted the black smudges under her eyes. She glanced up when she saw him waiting on the step, giving him a half-curiuos, half-searching glance.

'Good morning, Miss Montago,' Shelby said, and then felt at a sudden loss for words.

She gazed at him gravely now, not helping him, content to await his explanation.

'I came to see how you were—' Kent said awkwardly and then smiled and drew out his Bull Durham, recollecting himself so that he shoved it halfway back into his shirt pocket.

Isobel Montago's mood softened. 'Smoke if you want to, Mr Shelby. Perhaps you would care for a cup of coffee?'

She led the way inside the neat school-house and immediately set coffee to boil on the stove which was still alight from early morning. She spread a check cloth over the kitchen table and proceeded to lay places

51

for them both, fetching plates and knives from a cupboard and a dish of cold meat-pie.

'Will you have something to eat, Mr Shelby?'

He shook his head. 'Just the coffee, if you please. You go ahead. I guess you've got an afternoon class presently?'

She nodded and poured out the coffee, drawing a chair for herself and indicating one for Shelby.

'I guess so. Perhaps I should take Donna's advice and have a rest–'

'Miss Montago,' Kent began. 'You don't still figure I had any connection with those men?'

The smoky-blue gaze was level and fixed for a few moments; at last she shook her head.

'I guess if I really thought that, Mr Shelby, you wouldn't be drinking that coffee!' She laughed shortly and without humour. 'I admit I jumped to conclusions. I was a little hysterical. As soon as I heard the shots and saw you near that – outlaw, I thought of Johnnie in the Express office.

'I'm glad you shot Armstrong and I only hope the other two will be brought to justice, but I doubt it! Not that anything will bring Johnnie back, but men like those – killers are not fit to live.'

'Perhaps we'll have our chance later on to

settle with them,' Shelby said quietly, remembering the one thing he had not told the sheriff, namely that one of the bandits had ridden a grey-and-white horse with unusual markings. Kent felt certain that he would know the rider again if only by virtue of the horse he was riding.

'Did you know,' Shelby asked the girl, 'that Mason Hale of Horseshoe had been trying to buy Sugar Loaf from Gus Garner?'

Isobel Montago sipped her coffee and Kent saw that she had left the food almost untasted.

'In a vague sort of way,' she said. 'You hear all sorts of rumours in a place like Warpath. Some of them you accept, others you reject, according to your interest, I suppose. But I do know that Gus Garner hated Mason Hale and I'll tell you why. I don't know the details, as it all happened before I came to Warpath, but I do know that Garner had a son, a boy of about fifteen called Bob. It has been said, and probably with some truth, that it was through Mason Hale's carelessness that Bob was killed. There was something about a spring-wagon which Bob had to drive for some reason and Hale insisted on trying out two colts who had never been properly gentled and certainly had not been trained to wagon-trees and harness. They bolted and Bob was thrown and killed. I guess Garner never forgave Horseshoe for that. The only one he was even polite to afterwards was Donna.'

Shelby was following a specific train of thought.

'Do you remember, Miss Montago, whether Johnnie had mentioned to anyone his intention to try and buy Sugar Loaf?'

She sat a moment, lost in thought, striving to understand the significance of the question apart from the aspect of answering it truthfully.

'Why, I guess it was no secret that Johnnie intended to get a small spread,' she began hesitantly, 'but I'm wondering whether folks knew that it was Sugar Loaf he had in mind. No doubt he mentioned it to Garner himself and perhaps Donna. The three of us, Donna, Johnnie and I, have always been friendly. There aren't a great many young people of our age in Warpath or the valley.'

The girl rose presently and swept the things away into the cupboard. The crocks she set in a sink and poured water on them from the kitchen pump.

Shelby rose and thanked her. 'If I should ever get a line on those two men, Miss Montago, you can rely on me to bring them in–'

'Thank you, Mr Shelby, but I'm not too sure about Vern Hanson and Judge Winter–'

'You mean, they're crooked?'

'I'm not sure. I wouldn't care to say outright, but I've seen some funny examples of "law" in Warpath since I've been here. So have other folks too, I reckon.'

'What about the sheriff?'

'I am sure Tom Borden is straight enough. At least as far as I know. It's a pretty difficult chore, being a lawman in the west, Mr Shelby. But perhaps you know that?'

Kent nodded. 'I've known cases of honest enough men being forced by someone to do crooked things for fear of their wives or kids being made to suffer, or some such thing.'

She nodded. 'That's what I mean. If Borden *is* crooked then I'm sure it's because someone bigger than him, bigger than the law, is forcing him to it. As to Vern, I'm pretty sure he's prepared to do anything to feather his own nest. These are only my private opinions, Mr Shelby.' Isobel Montago smiled. 'They are not for publication.'

Shelby grinned. 'They won't be printed or even discussed, Miss Montago, but you've given me something to chew on.'

The schoolteacher picked up a large bell and crossed from the house to the school.

'I shan't have a class on Tuesday. That's the day of Johnnie's funeral. Thank you again, Mr Shelby, for coming and talking to me.'

He shook hands with her and turned on his heel, coming out on to the street and threading his way through the traffic to

Zwight Fuller's Grand Hotel saloon.

'Charlie,' Kent said, 'you stick close to the house and keep that carbine of yours handy. We're going to take a look at the range. I'll be fixing to cut out a small trail herd in a week or two if the young stuff's in good shape.'

Colfax nodded, turned back into the house and reappeared a few moments later with his carbine. He chose a rocker set at an angle on the veranda that would preclude the possibility of his being seen by riders approaching through the twin buttes.

Shelby built a smoke and Cal Eddy came up with the two saddle-horses.

'Be back by sun-down,' Kent called, thrusting his own carbine into the boot and mounting the sorrel.

Colfax, chewing on his tobacco, lifted a sun-burnt hand in acknowledgment and watched the two riders set off on a tour of inspection.

Shelby fished into his shirt pocket and drew out a piece of paper on which was a roughly sketched map in black ink.

'This was along with the title papers, Cal,' he said. 'Shows where Sugar Loaf range starts and finishes. Look,' he continued, pointing to the map with his finger. 'There's Dismal River that we cross by the military road out of Warpath. There's Horseshoe beyond those twin buttes which with their low hills marks our northern and Horseshoe's southern boundary.'

Cal nodded, frowning thoughtfully at the map. 'These yer hills to the north-west, that's where the copper mines are located. Plumb interestin' this,' Eddy continued; 'gives you a chance to see where yore neighbours are without the chore of havin' to visit 'em.'

'There's a spread known as Silvester's Pothook east of Horseshoe and down here, west of us, is Flying Wagon Wheel.'

Shelby took back the map and returned it to his pocket.

'I guess we know more or less what's ours now and what isn't. There's a line-cabin marked over to the eastern dunes descending from the twin buttes. I reckon we'd best give that a look-over, Cal. No telling when we might want to use that cabin when we start rounding up and branding strays.'

Eddy nodded and the two Sugar Loaf men put their horses to the cavalry routine of fifty minutes trotting and ten minutes resting.

Even so it took them nearly two hours to fetch up at the low grass-and-shale-topped dunes which flowed down on either side of the twin buttes.

Now and again, on those outer edges of Sugar Loaf land, stands of cottonwoods and live-oaks appeared and occasionally, particularly south of Dismal River, mesquite trees and clumps of chaparral brush showed up as blue-grey smudges against the steely glare of the desert beyond and to the south.

Cal Eddy suddenly reined his mount sharply and pointed to a low fold in the dunes ahead. Shelby's gaze followed the direction of Eddy's outstretched arm. Faintly he made out the thin spiral of smoke ascending into the afternoon sky.

Now Shelby withdrew the map once again and oriented himself. Returning the piece of paper to his pocket he turned his gaze to Cal Eddy's questioning face.

'That's where the line-cabin is right enough, Cal,' he said. 'Seems like someone's making good use of the shack.'

Eddy drew his six-gun, thumbed back the hammer and spun the cylinder. 'This is where we start in slinging lead—'

'No,' Shelby said. 'There may be quite a good reason why someone's using the shack. A lone traveller or foot-loose cowboy's got a range-right to do that; you know that, Cal, as well as I do. Don't let's go off half-cocked. We'll leave the horses over in that wash-out, yonder, and come up nice and quietly on the cabin.'

Cal reluctantly agreed and, ground-hitching the horses, the two men proceeded on foot until they had reached the entrance to the fold in the dunes. Eddy's six-gun was drawn and ready. Shelby had brought the carbine from the sorrel's boot.

Ahead they glimpsed the line-cabin set picturesquely in the grassy hollow. The washes sloped gently upwards on three sides, for the height of perhaps thirty to forty feet. The cabin was completely hidden from the flatter surrounding range. It was a natural hiding place.

Shelby started to walk forward then, the carbine in the crook of his arm. He stopped suddenly as he caught sight of the two horses grazing behind a few scrubby bushes. One was a dark roan, the other was a grey-and-white horse with unusually regular markings.

The last time Kent Shelby had seen that horse had been on Sunday morning in Warpath, when two masked bandits had fled from town with the proceeds of the Wells-Fargo Express pay consignment across their saddles!

Chapter IV

A Message By Donna

A second or two after Kent Shelby had spied the two grazing horses, one of them raised its head and nickered. Suddenly a man filled the open doorway of the cabin and westering sunlight glittered on the gun in his bunched right fist.

He shaded his eyes against the sun's oblique rays and sprang down from the steps, running forward in a half-crouch, making for a pile of dead-wood from where his six-gun would do more good.

Shelby had levered a shell into the carbine's breech and even as the man dodged and weaved in an effort to reach the protection ahead, Kent fired a warning shot, shouting to the man to throw down his gun.

But Shelby had given him the few precious moments he had needed and now from behind the dead-wood he fired, well within effective six-gun range.

Kent heard the scream of bullets tear the air uncomfortably close and then Cal was throwing down with his Colt, cursing as a bullet ripped into his shirt, branding his side with its burning-hot lead.

Kent threw the carbine up then in a sudden fury and smashed his nine remaining shots in and around the outlaw's flimsy protection.

The Sugar Loaf men saw two things happen quickly at once. The outlaw teetered on his heels and fell with a crash to the ground. A second man meanwhile had appeared near to the horses and was already astride the grey-and-white one.

Shelby's hammer clicked on an empty shell and with a grunt of disgust he ejected the cartridge case.

Cal sent two shots in the direction of the horses but the range was too far for a six-gun and already the man was lashing the beast into a racing gallop.

'Get him, Cal!' Shelby said, wiping a smear of blood from his cheek where a splinter of stone had cut a thin, jagged line.

Eddy ran fast towards the horses, as fast as any ranny could run in high-heeled boots and over rough rangeland.

In a few minutes he was racing past, sweeping through the opening towards the cabin. Shelby watched until he had disappeared along the narrow trail to the rear of the building.

He had no worry about Cal when it came to riding down another man or shooting straighter than most. Ten years or so ago

Eddy had been riding with Stonewall Jackson's brigade when the Confederate General, Joseph E. Johnson, turned defeat into victory at Bull Run by reinforcing Beauregard with his Shenandoah army. Cal Eddy, like many another Johnny Reb, had left the field literally covered in blood and no little glory; and Eddy was as good today at fifty, Shelby figured, as he had been then as a troop-sergeant of forty!

Kent now punched fresh shells into his carbine and walked towards the stiffly sprawled body of the outlaw. There was no shred of doubt in Shelby's mind that this one and the rider Cal was chasing were the same two who had gunned down Johnnie Montago and had taken the miners' pay.

He stirred the lifeless body with his foot. 'That's number two, Johnnie. In a little while we'll have the last of the bunch!'

He bent down and went through the dead man's pockets. Amongst a heterogeneous collection of articles was a roll of bills amounting to nearly three hundred dollars!

He placed everything back where he had found it, straightened up just as a distant shot echoed across the range.

Shelby rolled and lit a cigarette and then picked up the carbine and making for his horse he led it back towards the cabin, where he left it loosely tied to a post.

In spite of his confidence in Eddy he would

be worried and fidgety until the stringy little man showed up.

The fact that the door to the shack had stood open for some time was not, in itself, sufficient to have dispelled the liquor fumes and tobacco smoke. Against that background of smells was the raw odour of stale, unwashed bodies and Shelby violently shoved open the two windows.

The bunks were a tumbled mass of dirty blankets. Canned food had been opened and the empty cans thrown with a vandal-like disregard for anything decent.

On the rough, pine table lay the remnants of a meal over which the buzz-flies crawled and satiated themselves.

Shelby with a sudden wave of revulsion swept the congealing, half-finished meal in the stove, pouring kerosene on to firewood to burn the stuff and get rid of the smell.

He looked around for a broom and pail, filling the latter from the nearby stream. Then he returned to the shack and swabbed the floor and finally threw the dirty blankets out on to the grass.

He moved to the rear of the building now and laid his gaze across the brush-dotted washes. Less than half a mile away Cal Eddy was coming in leading a white-grey horse. Across the saddle Shelby could see the shape of a man jogging up and down with the grotesque movements of a puppet. A thin smile touched Kent Shelby's lips and for a moment he had that bitter satisfaction that always came when he had meted out his own brand of justice instead of waiting for the slow and often crooked hand of the law to move.

'Prisoner got shot tryin' to escape,' Cal grinned, sliding from leather and pulling the second dead outlaw from the white-grey horse.

'I heard a shot, Cal. Was that all it took?'

Eddy shook his head and the lean, brown face crinkled. 'Guess you didn't hear the rest then, Kent. The fust was his! He tried a snap-shot when he saw I was on the better hoss. We travelled some after that and then he tried again as I closed in. Two-three slugs come close enough to shave my whiskers an' that made me almighty mad so I dropped him with the Colt at about twen'y-five yards.'

Shelby nodded. 'These men may or may not have been working on their own, Cal. I've got an idea, but it's too hazy yet to go into. The point is, these two pilgrims were the men I saw taking the money on Sunday morning. There isn't any doubt about that. That evens things up for Johnnie Montago.'

'I went through his duds before packin' him on the hoss,' Eddy said rolling a cigarette and lighting it. 'The usual stuff except fer nigh on three hundred dollars!'

Kent's glance lifted and his eyes grew thoughtful.

'That makes two of them, Cal; but Curly Armstrong had but a few dollars in his pockets. It almost looks as though these two have been paid out for their part in the robbery.'

'Which means they didn't plan it themselves, Kent, otherwise the money would be here. That kind allus does hang on to it!'

'That's what I was figuring, although I haven't been through the cabin with a tooth-comb yet.'

'I figger yo're right, Kent. I'll lay a month's pay we don't find no miners' pay here.'

A half-hour later the two Sugar Loaf men closed the cabin door and pointed their horses to the home buildings. Each man led a horse and over each saddle was slung the body of an outlaw.

While Kent Shelby and Cal Eddy were visiting the line-cabin on the Sugar Loaf spread, Mason Hale was sitting in the small, untidy office which led off from the large living-room of the Horseshoe ranch-house.

Now the communicating door was firmly fastened against the possible advent of Donna or one of the servants.

Chip Bander watched his boss uncertainly, yet was able to savour to the full the rich, aromatic flavour of the cigar which Hale had offered him from the silver humidor.

Mason Hale was a big, craggy man whose rock-like face and physique was only now, in recent months, softening and rounding under the weight of superfluous flesh.

His piercing blue eyes, though not as pale as those of his foreman, were even more stone-like in their quality. His face was heavier of late and now more drink-flushed than Chip had seen it before.

The iron-grey hair was cut close and the bull-like head squatted on a short, thick neck that at times all but lost itself as the powerful shoulders rolled and hunched themselves in a sudden decisive gesture.

A bottle of whisky and a half-empty glass stood on a table at Mason Hale's elbow and now he heaved his enormous bulk to one side and drained the glass at a single gulp.

'You seem to have made an unholy, goddam mess of everything, Chip, don't you?' the harsh voice grated.

'*We* have, you mean,' Chip Bander said coolly. 'It was yore idea to trail Garner an' get the title deeds off'n him, but you didn't say what to do if some goddam pilgrim like Kent Shelby got there fust.

'Only we didn't know about Shelby then, so we left the drunken bum to fall into the creek, figgering that as the deeds weren't on him and that instead he'd got a roll of twen'y thousand, figgering then, like I say,

66

that he'd done gone an' sold to Johnnie Montago.

'I brought back that info, boss, before Borden or anyone knew about Garner, so then you fix for me to git Curly, Bessemer an' Cassel to hi-jack the miners' dough an' settle Johnnie at the same time. That way we kill two birds with one stone. If Garner ain't got the deeds et seems likely rumour is right fer once an' he's sold to Johnnie to spite you. You git the money all right but like Bessemer an' Cassel said, Johnnie didn't have the deeds. And why? Because by then, Mr Kent Shelby's come on the scene an' we hear *he's* the owner of Sugar Loaf.'

Hale sat and glared, puffing at his cigar. In his heart of hearts he knew Bander was right. They had moved fast, incredibly fast, but unknown and undreamed-of factors had been against them from the start.

'We done our best, boss, you know that, an' Chip Bander ain't makin' excuses. Nobody could've figgered thet Gus would've sold to the fust drunken *hombre* he met in Three Forks. Now, I guess we gotta think of somethin' else, an' anything that hurts Mr Kent Shelby'll do me a power of good!'

'We'll forget about what happened in the past, Chip,' the harsh voice broke in, 'and you can do what you like to Shelby so long as I get Sugar Loaf. I need a lot more money yet, Chip, for the plans I've got for me and you and the boys, and that miners' pay-roll wouldn't take us half-way there. It's Sugar Loaf with its rich copper deposits or nothing!

'Why, man, think of it. We've got everything laid on. Miners at hand, stamping mills only a few miles away. I tell you, Chip, if we can get that spread and open up that land we'll be rich beyond our wildest dreams!'

'How do you figger it's so good?'

Hale smiled. 'That dam' fool Garner let it out once in an unguarded moment. Donna told me. That's the only damn' good thing that girl's done in years.'

Chip Bander's eyes momentarily narrowed but the ramrod was smart enough to keep his mouth shut.

'You say you've given Shelby twenty-four hours to get off the place and take eighteen thousand for it,' the Horseshoe owner said.

Chip nodded. 'Said you might even raise the ante to twen'y if they went nice an' quiet. If not, we're goin' to give him a working over, and if we cain't drive him off then he'll go feet fust!'

'All right, Chip, but don't take too long over it. Time is precious and my schemes won't wait indefinitely.'

Hale rose from his chair to signify that the interview was over but the foreman stood there waiting.

'What is it, Chip?'

'Vern Hanson's getting troublesome, boss. Says his share ain't enough fer the risks he takes.'

'What's he get?'

'Fifty a month.'

'Make it seventy-five, Chip, and later on I'll settle with him in my own way.'

Even the cold, tough ramrod shivered slightly as he looked into the evil eyes of the man in front of him.

Bander's lids dropped quickly to mask his feelings. He even grinned as he turned and strolled from the room.

Charlie Colfax saw them coming in across the range, his sharp eyes noting the two led horses with their burdens slung across saddles.

He went inside the house, threw fresh, dry wood on to the stove and set the coffee-pot atop. Then he lit the lamps inside the house and hung a hurricane lamp at the doorway on the veranda.

Dusk was rolling in as Kent and Eddy came into the yard. Colfax watched from the step, a question in his black darting eyes.

'Had some trouble?' he called, unable to contain his patience any longer.

Eddy grinned. 'It was these jaspers as had the trouble, Charlie. Found 'em at our line-cabin on the eastern boundary.'

Colfax's gaze slid to Shelby's face.

'These two men escaped after the shooting on Sunday,' Kent said. 'Knew them by the white horse here, and when we reached the cabin they tried to make a fight of it. Reckon we'll have to take them into Warpath tonight. You come with me, Charlie. Let Cal stay here till we get back.'

'I ain't tired, Kent,' Eddy snorted.

'Cawfee's jest about ready if you wanta stop for it,' Colfax said.

Shelby nodded and slid from the saddle, drawing the reins over the sorrel's head. Cal dismounted and squatted tiredly on the porch steps. Colfax brought the hot coffee out in large mugs and they sat on the veranda drinking, smoking, talking, and watching the first stars appear in the darkening sky.

Shelby would not stop for long. He wanted to get this chore over with and inside of an hour Colfax and he were coming into town, making a detour through alleys and unlit side-streets.

Kent dismounted before they reached Main and left Colfax with the horses and the two dead outlaws. There was a light burning in the sheriff's office and Shelby thrust himself forward through the press of evening traffic towards it.

Tom Borden's glance came up as Kent entered the office, closing the door behind him with a scuffed boot.

'Hallo, Shelby.' The greeting was neither warm nor frigid, just coldly distant as though the speaker were a little unsure of himself, or perhaps unsure of the big man who stood before him. He waved to a chair and Kent lowered himself into a battered rocker.

'What's the trouble, Shelby?' Borden said, selecting a cigarette from a freshly rolled collection on the desk.

'Two more dead men,' Shelby said softly and felt the faint edge of amusement as Borden half started from his chair.

'The same two who stole the miners' pay and shot down Johnnie Montago when they rode in with Armstrong, Sunday morning.'

'You brought them in? Dead?' Borden's voice bore traces of surprised irritation.

Kent Shelby nodded. 'They were on Sugar Loaf, making a hide-out for themselves in our eastern line-cabin. Cal Eddy and me came up. I shouted to one of them to throw down his gun. He nearly killed me. I shot him. The other one didn't hang around. He grabbed a horse, the same white-grey one he rode Sunday, and lit out. Eddy went after him. He saved the county the expense of a trial–'

'What makes you think you can go around killing folks and bringing 'em in dead with nothing but your own story to back up a self-defence plea, Shelby?'

Kent stood up. 'Now I'll ask you a couple

of questions, Borden. Just which side of the fence are you on, and how many times does a man have to be shot at around here before he is morally and legally entitled to draw in self-defence?'

Borden's face went a deep roan colour. His mouth opened but Shelby was not through.

'You've had Curly Armstrong on a plate, sheriff. Now you've got the other two killers. Some law officers would be kind of grateful for that sort of co-operation from an ordinary citizen–'

'I ain't dead sure you *are* an ordinary citizen, Shelby,' Borden exploded. 'Mebbe you are – mebbe you're a little too free with that forty-five of yours–'

'Listen,' Shelby said coldly. 'I'm normally a patient kind of man, but within a little over twenty-four hours I've been shot at and nearly killed on my own land, and have been threatened by some of the Horseshoe H crew if I don't get off my own spread and quit the country!

'What kind of place is this, Borden, where a man is not allowed to run his own cattle without threats and warnings? 'Pears to me we could do with a little more law and order–'

Borden glared angrily, breaking in on the other's words.

'First I've heerd about you bein' threatened, Shelby. You ain't come in here before an' told me. You ain't asked for the law's protection, have you?

'Even a sheriff don't know everythin' that's goin' on around him,' Borden continued, 'and I ain't no mind-reader. If you've got any complaints to make about Horseshoe H or anyone else, or figger yo're bein' threatened, then it's your duty to let this office know an' if you need protection then it's our job to supply it!'

'Fair enough, sheriff,' Shelby said. 'What happens when you're not around?'

'If I'm not here, Vern Hanson is. He's got full authority to act in my absence. You got any trouble, Shelby, we'll work it out with a star instead of a gun.'

'I sure hope that star's big enough to shield us both from hot lead, sheriff!' Shelby grinned. 'What about the pilgrims outside? You want for me to take them down to Shilo's funeral parlour?'

Borden nodded. 'I'll come with you, just so you don't get crowded on the way!'

There was a light in the schoolhouse beyond the square and Shelby moved down the board-walk and descended the steps at the end before recollecting himself.

He cared little enough for the opinions other folk had concerning himself, but he guessed that talk and rumours would spread

73

like an ugly stain if he went visiting Isobel Montago at night.

He leaned against the clap-board building, fashioning a cigarette, his gaze probing, watchful, as though he were trying to discover something.

Riders came into town, singly and in groups, and the high gusto of their talk and laughter rang out over the noise from saloons and the hum of conversation and the echo of boots on the plank-walk. A few miners drifted in, some on horseback, others in rigs or spring-wagons from whose owners they had cadged a lift.

Black, indigo, mauve, and purple shadows moved as men drifted past open doorways and windows that threw bright yellow light into the stirring dust and movement of the street.

Shelby saw the bigger patch of light as the schoolhouse door opened and then closed. A slight figure was silhouetted against the night as it moved gracefully across the square towards the nearest steps of the board-walk.

For a moment Shelby thought it was Isobel Montago and then, as the woman came nearer, he made out the low-crowned stetson, the flash of white from the blouse, part-covered by a loose coat of some dark material.

She was almost on him before she saw him, or sensed his presence, and with a deep-throated exclamation, half surprise, half apology, she stepped aside.

'Good evening, Miss Hale – Donna,' Shelby said and watched the quick upward curving of her red lips as she recognized him.

'It must be fate, Kent,' she laughed. 'Do you know that I was looking for you?'

He shook his head. 'It's quite by chance I'm in town. You might've looked all night.'

The black hair glinted as she moved her head negativing his remarks.

'I was coming in to Sugar Loaf, Kent, to tell you Chip said father would like to see you – tonight. When I said I was coming into town to see Isobel, Chip asked if I would ride on and give you the message. I intended going on from Sugar Loaf the way you first came in–'

'Between the twin buttes?'

'She nodded. 'Of course, if you had been ready and had condescended to ride with m, I would have accepted your offer–'

Shelby grinned. 'We can ride back whichever way you say. You're the scout around here. But first I figure we ought to eat. Do you think we should give Warpath something to chew on as well, by having supper together?'

'Warpath can chew to its heart's content,' Donna said coolly. 'It wouldn't be the first time that the Hale name has been kicked around.'

'I wouldn't want that,' he said. 'Leastways not the name Donna Hale.'

'Wouldn't you?' she said and dropped her gaze for a moment, inexplicably embarrassed.

Shelby threw down his cigarette and stepped on it. 'Charlie Colfax is in the bar. I'll have a word with him. Then we can eat and hit the trail for Horseshoe.'

Chapter V

'You Had It Coming, Shelby!'

It was still early, a little after eight-thirty, when they pushed aside empty plates in the crowded restaurant of the Grand Hotel.

Shelby's black brows lifted as he reached for his makings and Donna nodded and smiled.

'Go ahead, Kent, I like the smell of tobacco with a man.'

He grinned. 'I guess you'll never grow into one of these fussy old spinster dames who cain't abide the smell of a cigarette or a drink.'

'Reckon not, Kent. I was raised on a ranch, don't forget, and apart from the servants I've been the only woman there since my mother died years aback when I was too small to remember. I guess they get to forgetting you're a woman, generally speaking. I've always ridden with the boys when I've felt like it, though it's a funny thing, Kent, they never let go their language in front of me.'

'I guess that's one thing to be said for most men, however much they swear, they almost

77

always respect the opposite sex, though Chip Bander – that's his name isn't it? – strikes me as being a man who would only have ethics and principles when it suited his book. Or am I treading on dangerous ground?'

She shook her head. 'I think maybe you are right, Kent. For a long time now I've been uncertain about Chip, and Dad as well for that matter–'

She caught herself up quickly and smiled away the question in his eyes, rising from the table and indicating the clock on the wall.

'If you want to get home tonight, Kent, we'd better be moving. Fortunately it's a beautiful, clear night. The stars are out in their millions – look–' she said as they moved out on to the board-walk, 'there's a moon coming up over yonder. We'll have plenty of light to see our way to Horseshoe.'

Both horses had been left in the livery barn and in a few moments saddle-girths were tightened and the mounts ready for the trail.

They crossed the Dismal by the military road and headed north-west over the range in the direction of Horseshoe.

Across the undulating land, the scent of sage came to their nostrils, strong and heady. A cool wind rippled the bunch-grass, bearing with it the smell of cool, dew-kissed earth, the perfume of wild flowers and the song of insects and small prairie animals not yet ready for sleep.

Above, the dark sky was a backcloth, setting off the jewel-like magnificence of the millions of sparkling stars.

A short distance ahead, the wide trail converged to a bottle-neck running between rocks and clumps of chaparral brush.

Donna urged her pony forward to take the lead and as distance increased between the two single-file riders, Kent's horse threw up its head and nickered. But the warning came too late. The rope had already hissed through the air and settled swiftly and tightly around Shelby's upper body, effectively pinning his arms to his sides as the lariat was drawn cruelly tight in spite of the rearing sorrel.

Riders emerged now from the brush-choked and boulder-edged trail and a man shouted, 'Cripes, the girl's here, what–'

'Never mind that,' Chip Bander snarled, 'she's gotta know some time. Might as well be now! Fish! Take her back to the house.'

The rider who had roped Shelby had come forward, the end of his lariat securely tied to saddle-horn. There was no chance to make a break for it. Now the man tugged Kent's hands behind him and lashed them with rawhide thongs. Next he lifted the forty-five from Shelby's belt and finally jerked him from the saddle, pulling him along by tugging the end of the lariat.

Ahead Shelby saw a man catch the bridle of the girl's pony as she sought to neck-rein the beast. She screamed and the man called Fish struck her a savage blow across the mouth.

But to Shelby's bitter, slitted, gaze it was not really a savage blow. It was as fine a piece of play-acting as he had ever witnessed. Now to give added emphasis and realism Donna was shouting. 'Chip Bander! What are you doing? You cain't do this–' But her voice was suddenly cut off as Fish Wilder, his hand firmly on the bridle, rowelled Donna's pinto with his spurred boot.

Chip Bander emerged from the moonlit shadows, followed by two of his crew. The man with the lariat pulled his horse up suddenly and Shelby almost pitched backwards.

Chip Bander, Frank Minden and Ward Reeves slowly dismounted and trailed their reins, Bander slightly in the lead. He stopped two feet away from Shelby and smacked him hard across the mouth.

'You don't learn fast, Shelby, do you?' he said softly, 'You was given twen'y-four hours to get out of the valley–'

'According to my calculations, twenty-four hours isn't up till tomorrow morning,' Shelby said evenly.

'Who the hell cares about your calculations?' Frank Minden demanded with a grin that threatened to split his bearded face.

Chip Bander smiled. 'That's right Shelby, it's like you say. Pay no attention to Frank, he always was a rough man!'

Bander waited patiently for the laughter to subside. He had all the time in the world and he was enjoying himself.

'Supposing it ain't twen'y-four hours until tomorrow, Shelby. What then? Are you lighting out to night or are you still goin' to be around?'

'What difference would my answer make?' Shelby said quietly. 'Either way I'm in for a beating and you know and so do I. I'll tell you this much, though, Chip. You'll be sorry for it before I'm through with you and that two-timing girl.'

Bander's laugh was a deep rumble in his throat. He licked his lips savouring the situation.

'Yeah! I guess she gave you my message all right. Cute of her, wasn't it, Shelby? Only you're such a goddam dumb ox you couldn't see through it! As for your threats, Shelby, why, I guess you ain't in much of a position to make 'em and sure enough you won't be by tomorrow. Frank! Let him feel that gun-barrel of yours, gently!'

Frank Minden grinned and brought up the long-barrelled Colt, hitting Shelby across the cheek so that the gun-sight carved a ragged channel down his face, filling with blood immediately. Shelby staggered back and in the moonlight his face showed waxy and pale. But the grey eyes now burned black with hatred as his gaze swept the bearded man with the gun.

'All right, Frank,' he gritted. 'I'll know you next time–'

Minden laughed.

Chip Bander said. 'You had it coming, Shelby. You know and we know you're the kind that likes to do things the hard way. We're just helping you, that's all.'

Bander's huge fist drew back and came forward with the speed and force of a steam-hammer, connecting with Shelby's jaw and dropping him to the ground.

Lights danced in his head and before his pain-smeared eyes. He shook his head to clear it and was aware of the throbbing ache in his jaw and the hot pain from the jagged wound on his cheek.

Slowly, very slowly, his head came up. Then his legs answered the insistent call from the tired brain. Awkwardly he began to climb to his feet. It took three full minutes before he managed to stand, spraddle-legged, swaying drunkenly.

'You sure do like to do things the hard way, Shelby. Like I said before!' Bander's fist came out again. This time the blow landed with sickening force over Shelby's heart. His legs held up for a few minutes whilst he became a human punchball. Pain spread slowly over his body until it was one vast, tearing ache.

Something cracked where his ribs were and another blow descended on his face, flattening the nose and filling the eyes with blood and pain. This time he went down for keeps.

Vaguely he was aware of high-heeled boots kicking into his body. He felt, almost without pain now, as a sharp spur gouged his thigh from groin to knee.

Soon the only parts of his body that were not a bruised and aching bloody mass, were his hands tied tightly behind his back.

Gradually the intolerable pain subsided as a welcome blackness descended over him...

'All right, Frank. Reckon he's not far off done for. Let's git back to the house.'

Ward Reeves said, 'He's still breathin', Chip. You figger on leavin' him like that?'

'Better to half-kill him than finish him off, Ward,' Bander grinned. 'He won't get under our feet even if he sticks around. Reckon Mr Shelby won't move much for a week, even if he is found. If he ain't–' Chip Bander shrugged and turned towards his horse.

In a few moments Horseshoe's crew was lost in the shadows of the night and as the moon reached out towards the western sky, it poured a cold, silvery light on to the bloody, unconscious form of the man who had dared to fight for his own spread and in doing so had bucked the Horseshoe H.

The first pearl-grey haze of early dawn was diffusing the eastern horizon when Isobel Montago sat up in bed recollecting that today Johnnie would be buried.

It seemed incredible to think that the lively, gay youngster was no more. She would never see him again, no more hear his infectious laugh or glimpse the bright blue eyes crinkling with merriment over some little thing that should, by rights, scarcely make a body smile.

But then Johnnie, for all his twenty-five years, had always been a kid.

How he had longed for a ranch of his own. How he had talked and planned with his sister what would happen as soon as he had the *dinero* to offer old Gus Garner!

Isobel threw back the bed-clothes and pattered across the pine-wood floor in bare feet and gazed out of the window, through which she could see the dark shapes of the town buildings sprawled out before her in the half-light, and farther on the still darker shapes of undulating rangeland with occasional blue-black smudges denoting brush and trees.

Mists were still lying across the valley and stirring gently in vaporous streamers above the river and suddenly the girl felt an urge to ride out across the range that Johnnie had loved so well. She would kiss the soft, springing ground with her feet and breathe in the cool damp air as a kind of salute to the memory of her brother.

Today Johnnie's earthly remains would be buried for ever, ashes to ashes and dust to dust, but his spirit, free now and untramelled, would sweep across the valley, and he would watch her riding and know and understand that his sister loved it too.

Quickly she dressed and made her way round to the small, tin-roofed stable where they had always kept the two cow-ponies.

She saddled the steel-dust and pulled the bridle over its head. Isobel's divided skirt made riding astride easy, and in a few moments she was out of town, across the military road-bridge, letting the animal race and expend its high spirits.

The wind tore at her hair, tugging and loosening the pins until the red-brown coppery tresses were flying long and wild like the pony's mane and tail.

She paid no heed to direction, such was her mood. She felt sad and gay at the same time, bound and yet free, and wondered for a brief moment whether or not this was sacrilege. And then it seemed, almost, that she heard Johnnie's good-natured laugh and his tumbling words urging her to go on and live and not think too much about the dead, and a sound came up from a nearby clump of brush in a racking groan so that for a moment the girl was petrified and pulled the horse back on its hind legs.

The steel-dust had already slackened its pace and now it nickered sharply in the early morning air.

She saw the blood-soaked figure moving slowly, painfully along the ground, the arms apparently tied behind. He was trying to reach a fallen limb and it flashed through her mind, intuitively, that he would try to discover a sharp piece of bark or split branch which might serve as a knife to cut through his bonds.

In a second she was out of the saddle, trailing the reins and running forward to the ghastly figure, crawling, crawling.

She knelt beside him, swiftly hacking the rawhide strips on his wrist with the sharp knife taken from his belt.

The arms dropped lifelessly away from the body and for a thought-flash it seemed to Isobel Montago that the man had died.

It was then that she saw the sorrel, vaguely recognizing it as a horse she had seen before, recently. There was no canteen on her own saddle-horn and now she walked to the sorrel and gently spoke to it, bit by bit, gaining its confidence so that at last it pushed its dew-wet muzzle at her and she was able to reach the canteen slung from the saddle.

On winged boots she sped back to the man, unstoppering the flask and using her own bandanna to wipe away the mass of caked dirt and congealed blood.

As soon as his face was partially clean, she put the canteen to his lips. For a second his eyes opened and the girl felt a wave of horror at what she saw there. Then the lids came together and Kent Shelby's lips sought the flask as he gulped the cold, clean liquid into his bloody and parched mouth.

She dragged the flask away while his eager mouth still reached forward and recommenced the chore of bathing his face. The angry gun-sight wound caused colour to beat into her face and for a moment anger made her hands tremble.

She knew that Kent Shelby had been beaten up. This was no accident!

Most of the congealed blood had been wiped from his face, revealing now the purple-black bruises on the pallid skin. The jagged wound, however, was already closing up as Isobel threw the soaking-wet bandanna to the ground. Her own hands were bloody but she wiped them on the grass and in the dew-moist dust, cleaning them as best she could. Then she rested Shelby's head and shoulders against the fallen limb and set to work with a fierce eagerness to chafe his wrists and arms back into life.

The sun was well above the eastern rim, flooding down the valley like a river of transparent gold, before Shelby opened his eyes again.

He gazed for a long time at the girl and pain pressed its ugly shape into his eyes and face as his torn nerves began to react to the punishment of his body.

His smile was a ghastly travesty without humour, yet he made it, and she recognized it for what it was and the steel-like, indomitable will that forced his broken lips apart and compelled his voice to come out even though as a mere croak.

'Thanks, Isobel,' he said and the effort caused sweat to stand out on his face.

Slowly, very slowly, he flexed the muscles of his fingers and hands, gradually clenching and unclenching his fists and lastly moving his arms experimentally.

Relief showed for a moment in the pain-racked face and in the stony eyes.

'They didn't break my arms,' he muttered. 'They left my hands. That was a mistake—'

'Who did this terrible thing to you, Kent? Who did it? Tell me!'

His broad, battered lips moved a little more easily this time in a grim smile, a smile in which was reflected a world of promised retribution.

'Chip Bander and his crew,' he croaked. His glance moved over to the sorrel and she knew that he wanted something badly. 'What is it, Kent? Something in your saddle-bags?'

'Whisky,' he whispered and closed his eyes again.

She brought it to him, quickly, a woman giving herself utterly and unsparingly to succour a wounded and helpless stranger; a woman prepared, further, to make recompense for an earlier mistake.

She stood back almost aghast and watched the terrible battle that she knew had to take place inside a man like Kent Shelby. The battle between his iron will and his battered body.

She had been there a long time, she knew, dimly aware that the sun was crawling upward in a steel-blue sky, aware that the dawn mists had fled and that the dew had vanished in the sun's rays. Yet time stood still. Seconds and minutes meant nothing in their own little world where that battle was being fought. Already he had managed to get on to the dead limb, had fumbled with tobacco and papers, willing her not to interfere by the very force of his cold, grey gaze.

He spilled tobacco, and dropped the papers, painfully forcing his tortured body to bend, urging his aching arms to reach out and finally with a gasp that drew the breath from his body retrieving the makings while sweat rolled down his face and on to his shaking hands.

Again he managed a twisted smile. 'See?' it said, 'I knew I could make it. You watch!'

'Let me help, Kent,' the girl almost sobbed, reaching out her hands still stained and dirtied with his blood and sweat.

'I've got to do it, Isobel,' he said huskily. 'Cain't you see I'm making progress?'

'Why must you torture yourself when I can do those things for you, Kent?'

He shook his black head slowly and put his hard, stone-like gaze on the girl's white face. The cold eyes softened a little. 'You've been dam' good, Isobel. Dam' good. But I've got to fight this myself. I reckon I'm going to stand up when I've got this god-dam' cigarette going.'

Pain and pent-up fury roughened his voice and the words themselves were not so carefully chosen under these hard conditions.

He got the cigarette rolled somehow and licked the paper with a dirt- and blood-encrusted tongue. He stuck the quirly in his mouth, drained of strength yet drunk with achievement.

His hand came down slowly for the whisky bottle and claw-like fingers hooked round the flask, gripping and lifting it as though it were a five-hundred-pound weight instead of a half-empty pint bottle.

But he knew that right now the raw spirit was the one thing to give his will-power and his body the necessary strength for the chore ahead.

He hefted the bottle and lifted it to his lips, feeling the fire of the spirit burn his mouth and throat and course through his veins. Strength flowed in with the whisky and Shelby shook his head and wiped sweat from his face, letting the empty flask fall to the soft ground, watching it as it lay there as though there were some particular significance in the fallen, empty bottle.

Then he drew cigarette smoke down into his lungs and pain slashed his face and his hand caught at his body.

She came forward, arms outstretched to help him. 'Please let me help!' she whispered.

'Reckon I've got a busted rib among other things,' he said between closed teeth. 'There's a red-hot pain down there. Let me be, Isobel. Let me do it myself, but thank God you're here to help me. Thank God you came–'

'Am I helping, Kent?'

His broken mouth split in a grin that held some little warmth and humour.

'You're helping all right, Isobel. Just by being here. I've gotta do this now or I'll fall right down.' He laughed shakily. 'Sure I'll fall down maybe, but that isn't all. I'll fall in your esteem, in my own, maybe. I don't know. Hell! Shut your ears, Isobel, if not your eyes. Maybe I'll forget myself and swear!'

'Swear away, Kent, if it'll help you get on

your feet. I don't mind. What kind of a woman would?'

He had no ready answer to that and knew, in spite of whisky fumes in his head, that he was wasting too much breath in too much talk.

He put both hands down on the limb, one on either side of him, and pressed down, easing himself forward, striving to transfer the heavy weight of his body to his shaking legs.

His face worked and his teeth bit into the bleeding lips to hold back the pain.

Isobel turned away, her eyes wet, her own body feeling the gut-retching torture that Shelby was enduring.

She walked to the horses and saw to the cinch-straps, wishing that there was another flask of whisky. She picked up the canteen. There was still a drain of water in it. When she looked again he was standing on wide-spread feet, swaying slightly.

She came forward and placed one arm around his body. There was strength as well as gentleness in the support. The flask she held up to his mouth, trickling the last drops of water into his open mouth.

'Thanks,' he said at last. 'Can you bring the sorrel over here?'

'Of course. Are you going to ride?'

He nodded and she knew the futility of words or argument.

Chapter VI

Revelation

The journey to Warpath was a nightmare for both of them.

Each time Shelby's body started to sag, Isobel Montago leaned over to hold him, desperation lending her an almost supernatural strength.

They had found Shelby's battered stetson on the nearby scuffed earth and now the wide brim protected his drawn face from the heat of the sun.

Isobel Montago remembered that the funeral was at two o'clock and glanced at her pocket watch, surprised that it was as yet barely eleven-thirty. But then she had ridden out soon after four o'clock that morning, she reminded herself, and felt an overwhelming surge of love towards her dead brother. Had it been Johnnie's voice that had called her to ride the range he loved? she wondered.

What if that feeling had gone by unheeded? Isobel doubted whether Shelby would have lived unless some other chance traveller had stumbled across him.

Now, thank God, she had been instrumental in saving a man's life. It was almost as though Johnnie had lived again. In a way, he did, she had not the slightest doubt.

Charlie Colfax was skirting the town when his black gaze took in the two drooping figures.

With a curse he pushed the horse forward, coming up to the girl at a steady run.

Colfax's eyes were two bright question marks until he realized that the girl did not know him.

'I'm Charlie Colfax, ma'am. Me an' Cal Eddy an' Kent run Sugar Loaf. My Gawd! What's happened? Who done this, ma'am?'

'Horseshoe beat him up, Charlie. Leastways, Chip Bander, the foreman, and some of his crew. I found him betwixt Sugar Loaf and Horseshoe. Help me to get him to Doc Cleary!'

Shelby's eyes opened and focused on Colfax's face.

'Hallo, Charlie,' he said. 'You been looking for me?'

'You're dad-blasted right we bin lookin,' Colfax said. 'Since dawn. Never mind the talk now. Let's git you down to Doc Cleary's!'

Shelby nodded and the girl led the way through sidestreets where once or twice curious glances moved over them in silent wonder.

The doctor was in and Colfax helped

94

Shelby slide from the saddle while Isobel held open the front door of the cottage.

Kent's legs almost gave out and when Charlie flung out a long lean arm, Shelby winced. 'My ribs, Charlie,' he gritted and Colfax held his arms, taking considerable of Kent's weight, half supporting, half dragging him into the doctor's house.

'Get him up on the couch, mister,' Cleary said and Colfax took Kent's shoulders and upper body, exerting his wiry strength to the full.

Isobel lifted the booted feet with Cleary's assistance.

'Looks like he needs more whisky, Doc,' Charlie said and Cleary glanced up aggressively. 'That's for me to judge, my man,' he snapped. 'Still, mebbe you'd best get some. He's sure in pain and will be while I dress his wounds.'

Colfax said, 'I'll be right back,' and strode out of the house.

'Whatever has happened, Miss Montago?' Doc Cleary said. 'He looks like he's been kicked by a wild-horse herd, or a bunch of crazy steers. Come to think of it, you look like you need something to steady you yourself. Here!' Cleary reached for a bottle and poured some bright-looking liquid into a medicine glass. 'Drink that,' he commanded her.

The girl took the draught gratefully and

drank it. A little colour came into her cheeks.

'Thank you, doctor. Now I'm ready to help you with Kent Shelby–'

'No, no, Miss Montago,' Cleary expostulated, 'that won't be necessary, besides I–'

'I found him and brought him in, Doc. Maybe saved his life. I'd like to see it through even if you won't want my help!'

'Oh, I see! Well in that case – now let me have a look.'

Once started, Cleary dropped his rather pompous way and got to work with no little skill.

He pulled off Shelby's boots and grey socks and placed a screen round the bed while he sterilized and dressed the jagged spur wound on Shelby's thigh.

Colfax came in with a whisky bottle and Cleary forced a little of the fiery liquid into Kent's mouth while Isobel and Charlie supported his shoulders.

'You've given him some, I see, Miss Montago. Good. That should hold him for a little while. Now–'

Cleary bent to his work again. He found the fractured rib without much delay and proceeded to bind Shelby's ribs so tightly that the dressing became almost the equivalent of the modern plaster cast. Then he began to work on the battered, broken nose.

Once Kent groaned and his eyelids fluttered open. His face was putty-coloured and sweaty. Cleary nodded to Charlie and Colfax handed him the whisky bottle.

Time went by as the doctor worked. Occasionally Colfax or the girl would give a hand. Presently Isobel called to Colfax.

'You'd better get a message to your ranch, hadn't you?' she said.

'Why, yes'm, but I ain't leaving–'

'No,' Isobel shook her head. 'Terry Guyler will go. He's one of my friends. I'll go see to it.'

Thanks, ma'am,' Charlie said, slightly bewildered, but she was already gone from the room.

Cleary was affixing a long strip of plaster over Shelby's face wound.

'He'll have to sleep here a while, Colfax,' he said. 'He's got a lot of liquor in him and he needs sleep to combat the shock.' The doctor studied his patient for a moment, felt the pulse and the heartbeat. 'Guess you'll have to get him back to your ranch, though I'd rather he were not moved–'

'Shelby'll insist on gettin' back soon as he wakes up, Doc. But thanks for what you've done. Reckon I kin manage to get him back this afternoon.'

Clearly nodded. 'I'll keep him quiet here, even if he does come out of that drugged sleep. You come back about five o'clock. You can get him back to – Sugar Loaf, isn't it? – old Gus Garner's spread – before dusk?'

Colfax nodded and as he gazed down at the battered and bruised body, the black eyes burned with the fires of a hellish hate. The seamed face twisted and looking up Doc Cleary saw stark murder in a man's black eyes.

Straight from the cemetery on the hill, Isobel Montago made for home, throwing herself on to the bed and giving way to a fit of uncontrollable sobbing.

Slowly the tears subsided and presently she straightened up and walked across to the wash-stand, pouring cold water from a pitcher into a bowl.

She bathed her face and hands, feeling better now, already her mind working around the problem of Shelby.

Cleary had told her that Kent would not be moved until five o'clock. She had time then to find Colfax, to consult him and suggest what was in her mind.

Where would Colfax be, most likely? she wondered, and realised that the only way to find out was to go the rounds of the town, irrespective.

She tried the lobby of the Grand Hotel and then the restaurant, drawing a blank each time. Then she pushed open the doors to the bar, drew a deep breath and walked boldly in.

The hum of conversation died quickly as

men's surprised glances shuttled across to the trim figure of Warpath's schoolmistress.

Colfax saw her, saw the relief on her scarlet cheeks as he came forward, and, with a quaint gentleness for such a rough man, took her arm and guided her out into the lobby.

'Look, Charlie,' Isobel said. 'About Kent. Let me fix for a spring-wagon to take him back. Have you thought that he may not be able to ride a horse?'

Charlie Colfax pushed the sweat-and-weather-stained stetson to the back of his greying head.

'Reckon it's an idee, Miss Montago,' he said. 'Mebbe Kent won't be able to fork a hoss again for some time. How bad do you figger he is?'

The girl frowned thoughtfully.

'It's difficult to say, Charlie. With an ordinary man it would mean about a month in bed, I should say, with doctors and nurses. As it is – well, I reckon that Kent isn't an ordinary man, although he's got a fractured rib, a broken nose, and some nasty cuts and bruises. Still it wouldn't surprise me if he's riding inside of a week although he'll have to have those wounds dressed and all that bandaging around his middle until the rib's healed.'

Colfax nodded sombrely. 'When I git my hands on them, Miss Montago, they'll shore wish they never even heerd of Sugar Loaf.'

His gaze came away from the distance, back to her face.

'Kin you fix to have the wagon with plen'y o' straw at the doc's around five o'clock, Miss Montago?'

She nodded. 'Sure I will, Charlie, but listen to me. Don't you go off half-cocked about Horseshoe. Mind if I give you some advice? Then wait until Kent's able to talk to you about it. Together you might figure out something better than acting on your own.'

Colfax's lids drew back a little from the black eyes. 'Yo're smart, Miss Montago,' he grunted. 'Anyway it's a promise.'

Isobel Montago was as good as her word. Even before five o'clock the spring-wagon was waiting at the rear of Doc Cleary's cottage as Colfax came up on his horse leading Shelby's sorrel.

He touched his hat to the schoolteacher and slid from leather.

'The doc's ready for us,' she told him and preceded him into the house.

Once, during the afternoon, Cleary told them, the patient had awakened in some pain and the medico had administered something to quieten him.

Now as they lifted him into the well-padded bed of the wagon, his lids opened tiredly. He managed a faint grin and then seemingly lost interest in his surroundings.

'He sure looks like he's been in the wars,'

100

Doc Cleary remarked heartily. There was a white bandage across his nose and some stiffening that the doctor had put there in an effort to straighten the broken bone and help it knit straight, and half of the left side of his face was covered by surgical plaster.

'I'll be out to see him tomorrow or Thursday,' the doctor told Colfax. 'Meanwhile keep him in bed. On no account must he get up or move around until I say so. If he's troublesome tonight here's a sleeping powder. Drop it into a glass of milk and make him drink it.'

'Milk?' Colfax echoed, aghast.

'Yes, milk! Not whisky!'

'I'll come with you and bring the horses, Charlie,' Isobel said. 'Then I can drive the wagon back.'

He shot her a grateful glance and climbed up on to the seat. Behind, Isobel Montago rode the sorrel, leading Charlie's horse on a short rein.

They trailed along at a gentle, easy pace and still made the Sugar Loaf ranch-house before the sun had vanished in a blaze of crimson and gold.

Cal Eddy, prepared by Terry Guyler's message, had everything ready.

Kent was carried into his own room and placed on the bed. Cal fiddled with boots and trousers while Charlie brought coffee into the living-room for the girl.

She was looking at the gunny-sacks across the smashed windows.

Colfax followed her gaze with his bright eyes.

'That's somethin' else Horseshoe's goin' to answer for,' he said grimly, 'but that ain't nuthin' to what they done to Kent, nor is it nuthin' to what they're goin' to git–'

'But why, Charlie?' the girl demanded. 'Why are they hounding you, shooting at you?'

'Reckon they want us off'n Sugar Loaf land so's they kin move in. Kent says Hale's bin tryin' to buy fer some time but Garner wouldn't sell.'

'I know,' Isobel nodded. 'That's what Donna Hale told me. But why should Horseshoe want this small spread when they've got all the room in the world?'

Colfax shrugged. 'Some folks ain't never satisfied,' he growled. 'They git land-hungry an' power-hungry; they jest cain't satisfy their appetites. Kent figgers it might be on account of copper on our land.'

'Is there copper here?'

'We don't know,' Charlie grinned. 'Garner said somethin' about it but we ain't sure but what he was jest havin' Horseshoe on a string.'

'I see,' the girl said slowly, 'and as long as you and Kent and Cal Eddy stay here you're wide open to any dirty sort of trick that Chip or Hale want to try?'

'That's about the size of it, ma'am,' Eddy said, coming in from the kitchen to refill the coffee-pot. 'But they'll sure find we kin fight back.'

'Donna isn't in this, I'm certain,' Isobel said. 'She's my best friend, has been for years. Whatever her father, Mason Hale, or Chip Bander are up to, I am quite sure it's without Donna's knowledge.'

Eddy shrugged. 'Cain't say, ma'am. We ain't even met Hale. It's Horseshoe's crew an' foreman we're goin' to settle with fust!'

When the Horseshoe men moved out of the shadows, Donna pulled her mount in sharply. In the moonlight she recognized the darkly etched features of Chip Bander, Ward Reeves and Frank Minden. Shelby had been roped by Bill Gunn, she saw with a dawning horror. Then someone shouted and Fish Wilder came up out of the darkness and grabbed the bridle of her pony.

Donna tried hard to turn her mount. She screamed as Fish Wilder struck her savagely across the mouth.

'Chip Bander,' she cried. 'What are you doing? You cain't do this–', but her words were cut off sharply, in mid-sentence, as Fish Wilder kicked and rowelled her pony and sent it rearing and plunging forward across the range.

Fish still had hold of Donna's reins and almost hysterically at first the girl beat against him with her fists until she saw the utter futility of it all.

'I don't know what's behind this outrage, Wilder, but I'll soon find out and have the lot of you fired, along with your precious ramrod, Bander!'

Fish smiled evilly. 'Reckon yo're sure due fer some surprises, Donna–'

'How dare you call me Donna?' the girl flared, but Fish Wilder only grinned the more and tightened his hold on the reins, pushing his mount and urging Donna's pinto hard towards the Horseshoe ranch-house.

Mistily through tears of anger and shock at memory of Shelby's tied form, she saw ahead the dancing lights of Horseshoe.

Was this really her spread, her father's spread, to which she was being urged with indecent haste and violence? Was this rough Fish Wilder the same man who, the day before, had touched his hat and muttered, 'Good mawnin', Miss Donna'?

Could this nightmare of events be enacted with the cognizance, if not the authority, of her father?

The thought made her falter, almost, but Wilder half pulled her from the pony and forced her numbed feet to march across from the rack to the lighted doorway on the veranda.

It was like a dream. A horrible dream and yet she knew it was real enough. Wilder had gone and she was in the huge, familiar living-room. Faint curls of smoke ascended from the glowing logs in the fireplace before which her father stood, vast and forbidding, like a huge rock against which the seas of opposition would wash in vain!

She had never felt like that before. Never as though her father were a rock waiting there, immovable, for her body to smash itself in futile effort.

She watched the craggy face as it creased into a humourless grin. She knew it was without warmth or humour or affection because the eyes remained cold and wary, like Chip Bander's. That is if pale, wet stones can appear wary.

'It's time you understood a few things, Donna,' Mason said and his bluff heartiness was just another lie he was offering her.

'Sit down, while I talk to you, child,' he continued in his grating voice. And like a sleep-walker she moved to the nearest chair and sat without feeling the hardness of the seat or arms at her sides.

'I know what Chip was about, tonight, Donna,' Hale said, selecting a cigar and biting off the end.

'I half expected one of the boys might have to bring you home. Maybe they're settling with Shelby right now, I don't know. I don't much care. Chip can handle it his way just so long as he *does* handle it, and quickly! In a very little while now, Donna, Horseshoe's taking over Sugar Loaf whether you like it or not. If you want to stay and take your place here with me and the boys, you can. If you don't – well, the west can be pretty tough on a woman on her own, particularly a very lovely young woman!'

The green eyes widened still farther in shocked incredulity. Was it possible that this man who stood before her, the very personification of evil, brute strength, could be her father, even though she had never received the warm, generous affection that should have been her due?

He seemed to know what she was thinking and gave her his cold smile again.

'You're thinking that I don't behave much like a father, Donna, aren't you? Well maybe I haven't had much time for sentiment and soft words. I've been busy carving out an empire.' He smiled bleakly. 'A small one at the moment, it is true. But it will grow, particularly if you help me.

'I'll tell you something now, Donna. I took you in when you were a kid and your own father was a drunken sot who finished up in the gutter with a bullet in his back. Maybe this hasn't been a soft home for you but at least it's been a home. You've had food and clothes, a good education–'

'What are you trying to tell me?' the girl whispered. 'That my real father died a drunkard, killed, and that you took pity on me and brought me up?' The shocked horror in her eyes was naked for the man to see.

Mason Hale waved a hand in a deprecating gesture.

'Jim Russell and I were partners, in a small way, you understand, but Jim spent more than his own share of money in getting drunk most every night. I'll say this for him, though, he could use his fists. Could knock out most men with one blow, but it was obvious that sooner or later he'd get into some tavern brawl. In fact he got into several and I had the job of trying to smooth things out. I couldn't smooth the last one out, though, because Jim knocked a man out and killed him. Even though it was an accident the man's friends were after Jim's blood. Like I said, he was found shot in the gutter. There were no witnesses, no proof as to who had done it. Plenty of suspicion but not proof.'

'Why have you not told me all this before?' Donna said softly.

The big man hunched his massive shoulders as he sat down in a chair at the table.

'There was no reason to tell you until tonight, Donna,' he smiled. 'I saw Fish Wilder bringing you in and guessed that Chip was dealing with Sugar Loaf. Those drifters haven't any right there, Donna, don't you see? I made Garner a good offer for Sugar Loaf long ago. I even repeated the offer to Shelby. Why do they have ter come here out of all the places they could pick for a ranch? I want Sugar Loaf because there's minerals there that could be exploited, not because of the graze for a few hundred head of cattle. Now these saddle-tramps are standing between me and a fortune just so they can run a handful of cattle which they could do most anywhere else. Now do you understand?'

Donna swallowed hard. 'I'm grateful for the explanation fath – Mr Hale. I cain't understand why you took me in, kept me all these years. Didn't Dad have any relatives?'

'None that I know of.' Hale rose. 'Now then, Donna, you run along to your room. If I were you I'd keep off Sugar Loaf and steer clear of Shelby and his crew if you see them around. Somehow,' Hale murmured reflectively, 'I don't figure you'll see 'em around much more!'

Donna walked wearily up the wide staircase to her room, her mind dazed with the sudden turn of events. Why had such a man as Mason Hale bothered to saddle himself with his dead friend's daughter? Was it that underneath that craggy exterior the milk of human kindness flowed rich and thick?

And now what? She could either agree with or condone everything that Horseshoe did now, legal or otherwise, decent or wicked, or else walk out! Would Hale really let her walk out if she wanted to and were his last words intended in the nature of a warning not to go too far from the ranch, not to see or speak to Shelby or his hands?

Chapter VII

A Fly on the Window

Kent Shelby's swollen and bruised eyes opened slowly. In the greyness of early dawn he recognized, after a few moments' mental effort, familiar shapes.

He saw his clothes, neatly stacked on a chair, his gunbelt slung across the back. He could just make out the shape of the forty-five's butt as it protruded from the holster. The sight gave him some comfort, however bleak his feelings.

He became conscious now that his face and eyes and head ached intolerably and that his mouth was crammed with filthy waste of such absorbent quality as to have sucked every drop of moisture from his mouth. His lips must have bled again during the night, he thought, as he moved them and tasted the bitter flavour of half-dried blood.

Now he discovered that his mouth was not stuffed with cotton waste because he could, with great effort, move his tongue. He even managed to swallow and then he saw the carafe of water at the bedside table. The pain of his battered ribs slashed him as he moved his arm and upper body so that he began to ease his hand gently an inch at a time towards the flask of water and drinking-glass.

It was another game such as he had played in front of Isobel Montago, this seeing which was the stronger, his will-power or his body. But it was a grim kind of game, one that was as stripped of humour as a slaughtered steer is stripped of its hide.

By the time he had shakily slopped water to the brim of the glass and had drained the contents the room was appreciably lighter.

Small noises began to crowd into his clearing brain. Dishes and pans rattled somewhere inside the house and a man's booted feet moved deliberately and quietly across the kitchen down the hall.

The bawling of cattle came through the open windows, a soft, gentle sound, rendered more harmonious by distance. Like bagpipes, he thought with a grin, and surprised himself by that sudden smile.

The scent as well as the sounds of the range blew into his room and Kent Shelby knew in that moment, even though his body ached and his mind tortured him, that such things as a man's own place, perhaps with the right woman to share it, were, after all, worth fighting for. Worth even such a beating up as he had had, only that Kate Trafford had two-timed him and now Donna Hale, with her wicked green eyes and red mouth and cascading black hair, had coiled herself around his heart and then struck with the speed and venom of a rattler.

If Shelby had needed any confirmation of Donna's guilt he had found it in Chip Bander's admission. That the girl had deliberately duped him in asking him to come to Horseshoe. That Bander was such a man to trade on a misunderstanding of words, and derive pleasure from the evil created, even Shelby did not then appreciate.

But in spite of the whisky he had consumed and the vague and hazy recollections of being treated by a doctor, his brain or memory still retained the picture of Isobel Montago as she had helped him from the time of his dawning consciousness.

He began to plan, or to try and formulate some plan, whereby the running of the ranch could really start in earnest and Bander and his crew could be dealt with at the same time.

It started off with the question of manpower. If Cal or Charlie were to stay at the house – and for a time that would obviously be necessary – then it left only one of them for the back-breaking job of riding the range and cutting out a trail-herd of suitable three-year-olds. That was a chore that no one man could do on his own, even Cal or Charlie.

What then? One of them would have to go

into Warpath and bring in an outsider. A man who was prepared to fight as well as ride herd on cattle. A man who was willing to risk his life for forty a month. A man who offered, on top of all these other things, the one greatest attribute of all – loyalty!

Was there such a man? Shelby asked himself and knew the answer immediately. He had worked with such men, had ridden the trails with them, had shared chuck-wagon meals with leather-faced cowboys who coolly faced the lowered horns of a crazy steer as they did the muzzle-hole of an outlaw's forty-five. Yes, and all for forty a month! Loyalty was part of the cowboy's equipment, like his saddle and war-bag and mug and knife and fork. His gun was not equipment, it was part of him.

Why was there then such a deeply ingrained sense of loyalty among this wiry breed? Why were men like Chip Bander prepared to go to any lengths for the sake of their boss and their home ranch? And at the other end of the scale were men whose loyalty was of a finer kind. Men who had gone on working for their particular brands without pay, month after month, shrugging away their boss's embarrassed explanations and getting on with the chore at hand!

Well, all that meant that Cal would have to get at least one more hand. Cowboy, miner, drifter – Shelby could not afford to be fussy.

Then they would have to round up the herd, search out the low hills and river-brakes for mavericks and brand 'em before Horseshoe, or Pothook to the north-east, or Flying Wagon Wheel to the south-west, clapped their own brands on!

There was another thing Shelby intended to get done, although that could, if necessary, wait until later. He was determined to settle once and for all the question of whether or no copper existed under the range. He would have to get a pretty smart miner at least, probably a mining expert, but it would be worth the bother. One thing Shelby was quite resolved to do and that was to fight on, regardless of whether Sugar Loaf were wealthy in minerals or merely good grazing range.

Chip Bander and his crew were going to be sorry, Kent promised. Somehow or another they were going to be hurt until they screamed for mercy. But there wouldn't be any. Neither, Kent considered, would he find much pity or feeling in his heart if Donna also should have to suffer.

Such are men's thoughts in the bitterness of their own suffering and such are their intentions until time and events change the colour and shade, until patterns are no longer clear-cut, no longer black and white.

Shelby handed the empty plate to the grinning Colfax and reached gingerly to the table for his makings.

'Reckon Cal'll be glad you did justice to his breakfuss, Kent,' Charlie grunted, highly pleased. 'I'll take the plate an' fetch you some cawfee. You sure you're sure you feel better?'

Shelby grinned and nodded. 'I'll be up soon, you see!'

A look of alarm flickered into Charlie's black eyes. 'The doc done told us you ain't gotta move about, none, Kent. You gotta stay put till he says you're fit.'

'You talk too much, Charlie. Go get the coffee!'

Cal put his head round the door and said, 'Howdy, Kent. How you feelin'?'

'Better than yesterday,' Shelby said. 'Find me a shaving mirror, Cal.'

Eddy came in a few minutes later with a cup of coffee and a fly-blown shaving mirror.

Kent took the glass and stared at his own reflection. He did look pretty bad, he thought, although the doc had made a good job of patching him up, had even cleaned the dust and blood out of his hair. But no doctor could have prevented the yellow and black bruises from coming out or done anything about the white lines of pain around the broken lips, or stopped the skin stretching tightly on the face so that it had that scraped, bony look that comes to the face of a man or woman who has been through hell, either physically or emotionally.

'You figger you kin shave, Kent?' Eddy asked anxiously, seeking to interpret the changing expressions on Shelby's face.

'Yes, Cal. Make it snappy, will you?'

Before Shelby had finished the steaming coffee, Cal was back with shaving brush, soap, hot water and razor.

'Now leave me to it,' Kent said and Eddy slid from the room.

It was middle afternoon and hot. Shelby felt stifled in his room. The doctor had been and had expressed his surprise at his patient's 'recovery'. Not that he had used the word, of course, but Shelby figured he would not have been surprised to see a corpse.

Kent listened to the ticking of the cheap timepiece that Charlie had brought into the room. He watched the hands crawl by, wondering at times whether they were moving or whether it was his imagination. A fly crawled up the window pane, reached the top and dropped down again with a great deal of buzzing. Kent watched, fascinated. It did the same thing seventeen times and finally flew out through the top of the window.

Kent searched the recesses of his mind, recollecting that in some dim, distant period of history a guy by the name of Bruce had watched a spider in a cave.

Slowly he eased himself out of bed, placing his bare feet carefully on the pine floor. His head swam a little and his legs were rubbery, but that was little in comparison with the pain in his side.

He sat on the edge of the bed and looked at the clock. The hands pointed to a quarter after four. Charlie, he knew, was dong chores around the house and outbuildings, Cal had gone into town. Now was the time!

He found it easier to crawl over to the chair where his clothes were. Once there, he dragged the chair across the floor back to the bed. Then he sat back and wiped sweat from his face and waited for the pounding of his heart to subside...

Kent Shelby dragged on his boots and keeping his body as rigid as possible, lifted his gaze to the clock. The hands were pointing to ten minutes of five. But he'd done it, goddam it, he'd done it!

He heard the distant rataplan of hooves across the range, even as he swung open the door. His glance dropped to the gun-belt still on the chair and painfully, slowly, he buckled it on. The heel of his hand rested for a moment on the gun-butt and immediately he sensed the strangeness of it, recollecting then that one of Bander's crew had lifted his own forty-five. Either Cal or Charlie must have put this spare gun in his shell-belt.

Now he spun the cylinder and found five chambers loaded. He withdrew a cartridge from the belt and rammed it home into the chamber.

Re-holstering the gun, he started on his tottering way, slowly, step by step, traversing the hall until he reached the screen door opening on to the veranda.

He opened and closed the door, limping out on to the porch, blinking at the sun's oblique rays as they slanted across from the west.

Down by the corral he glimpsed Charlie Colfax, rifle in hand, waiting, and a scant hundred yards away the rider came tearing in, ahead of the rising dust cloud.

Colfax lowered his rifle as Donna Hale raced through the open gate into the yard. Dust and gravel shot upwards as she pulled the sturdy cow-pony to an abrupt halt.

Dust settled over everything and Shelby noted objectively that even with her face finely powdered with alkali dust, Donna Hale was still supremely beautiful.

She slid from the saddle as Colfax came forward and took the pony's reins. Then she cuffed riding skirt and legs with her stetson and suddenly her glance lifted and locked with Shelby's cold gaze.

She ran up the steps, breathless, her breast rising and falling sharply, her face, for all her riding, now strangely pale. She watched him limp to the veranda steps, saw the physical pain stab at him and watched the bitterness rise up to his scarred face from the very depths of his soul.

'Kent! My God, Kent! What have they done to you?' Her voice was rough with near-hysteria and Shelby marvelled at her supreme acting.

'You should know, Donna. You beautiful bitch. Didn't you take me by the nose and lead me straight into the arms of Chip Bander and his boys?'

For a moment he thought she was going to faint. Her face drained itself of what little colour there was, matching almost the whiteness of her blouse. In her eyes, those wicked green eyes, he saw stark horror. Then her eyelids fluttered down as though to shut out the picture in front of her.

'I'm not very pretty, now, am I, Donna?' Shelby said. 'Worse even than before. A scarred face, broken lips, broken rib, scarred leg and a few minor cuts and bruises–'

'Dear God,' she muttered, so softly that for a moment he scarcely understood. 'You must believe me, Kent. God make him believe me. I never knew about Chip Bander and his men. He said to tell you that father – that Hale–' she stumbled and went on, 'wanted to see you–'

'Chip said you knew. He said you were cute.' The voice cut into her low-voiced protestations like the stinging lash of a whip. He saw the eyes then like beautiful green stones in a sea of sparkling tears. She was close to him now and clutched his arms, looking up into his wooden face with naked misery in her gaze.

'You must believe me, Kent. I knew nothing, nothing. God, don't place me so low as that, Kent. Not to any living thing would I do such a thing. Not to my worst enemy, Kent, least of all–'

'Least of all, what?' His voice was a flat monotone, devoid of any rhythm, stripped of any warmth.

She dropped her hands and moved away as though the effort to convince him were too much for her strength.

Colfax came up then and brought a kind of sanity back to the situation. 'You want for me to make some cawfee, Kent? Hey! Reckon you'd best sit down an' take it plumb easy. You look kinda washed out!'

The tension in Shelby slowly eased and lessened. Charlie's brusque voice, his leathery face helped to bring a normality to things. Shelby almost smiled. 'Yes, Charlie, you do that.'

Colfax muttered into his whiskers and tramped round to the rear of the hut as Shelby, exhausted now, sank down into the rocker on the porch.

She drew a chair close to the rocker and

sat down, leaning her elbows on her knees, looking into his face with a kind of hopeless determination.

'Listen to me, Shelby,' she said, her voice low and vibrant. 'The night before last I was taken by Fish Wilder and struck across the face. You can still see the mark if you care to look, if you can see anything at all, Kent Shelby! Wilder manhandled me and forced me back to the house. I was half crazy with rage and fear for what they might be doing to you. I was going to fire the whole crew as soon as I saw my father! That's what I thought! Mason Hale knew, more or less, what was going on. He's letting Chip Bander play his own hand just so he drives you and your crew off Sugar Loaf.

'The joke is,' Donna went on, her eyes bright with unshed tears, 'Mason Hale is not my father at all. My pa was a drunken bum called Jim Russell, so Hale told me on Monday night, who died in the gutter full of liquor and a bullet. Hale was his friend, so he took me in. He didn't want to tell me all this, but things built up to a climax; this question of getting Sugar Loaf because it's supposed to have minerals–'

Shelby's grey glance lifted and fire burned deep within him, reflecting itself in his gaze. Not the fire of hatred and bitterness, but the fire of compassion and resolve.

'That means you're running your head

into a noose, coming here?'

She nodded and Shelby watched the last rays of the sun turn and spin their facets of light in her blue-black hair.

'One of them followed me from the house, but I managed to throw him off. I made for the hills and I know this country better than most of the crew.'

'Maybe you lost him, Donna, but that still doesn't make your position very good.'

'No, it doesn't. Hale said I could stay on there and be a good girl. Do what he said. Or else I could drift. He said the west was not very kind to a girl who drifted.'

'All this is true, Donna?' Shelby's voice shook a little, was uncertain.

She lifted her face and looked at him. 'As God's my judge, Kent. Everything was as I have told you!'

He took her hand, wincing slightly with the movement, but yet there was less pain in his eyes now.

'Can you forgive me for misjudging you so, Donna?'

'Forget it, Kent. I guess you've been through enough as it is. Now I'd better be getting back–'

'To what, Donna?'

She shrugged. 'I don't know. Maybe he'll treat me right. Maybe he'll look on me as a kind of prisoner. Protective custody, isn't it called?'

Colfax came out with two steaming cups of coffee. He squinted along the track to town.

'Riders comin', Kent. Mebbe Cal an' somebody. Mebbe not.'

Colfax moved off and Donna and Kent waited until the riders drew nearer, stirring the dust.

Presently Shelby said. 'It's Cal Eddy with a new rider. They're sure hitting the breeze.'

Donna stood up. 'There will be much dust over the valley before we can see peace ahead, Kent. I must go now. I will try to come again.'

'Soon?'

'Soon!'

Shelby stood and watched her ride towards the twin buttes. Once she turned in the saddle and waved. He lifted his arm and then Cal Eddy clattered into the yard with a small, thin man mounted on a first-class piece of crow-bait.

'This yer's Harry Busch, Kent. Harry this yer's Kent Shelby. Harry's workin' fer us, Kent!'

'Is he that crazy?' Shelby smiled.

Harry Busch looked hurt. 'Mebbe I don't look much, Mr Shelby, but you wait. You'll see.'

Chapter VIII

Trail-Herd

Dust did stir over the valley for the next week, but it was the dust of milling cattle and quick-running sure-footed cow-ponies. The dust of battle, Shelby thought grimly, would come later.

He was astride the sorrel and presented a different picture from the one of nearly a week ago. The bruises on his face were almost gone and the plaster had been stripped from the jagged, gun-barrel wound two days ago. It was drawing together well with the aid of a few stitches Doc Clearly had sewn.

Shelby's face had lost a great deal of its white, waxy pallor. Already the sun and wind was beating back the natural mahogany colour, but the bones were still prominent, the skin tightly stretched and the eyes darker than grey eyes should be.

Now and again he put the army glasses to his eyes and surveyed the range. Dust clouds occasionally appeared on the horizon to north and west, like smudges of yellow smoke. Cal Eddy, Charlie Colfax and Harry Busch had been sweating like demons for the last three–four days, from sun-up to sun-down. Twelve hours a day in the saddle with short rests for breakfast and the noon meal. Twelve hours a day under the burning July sun and time against them.

Already two hundred or so prime steers had been cut out and driven down to home pastures, but unless the men could finish their job quickly within the next few days, these fat steers would drift and scatter, seeking perhaps the more succulent grasses down by the river or roaming back to the parts of the range from which they had lately been driven.

Shelby was content to stay near the house for the time being. There would, he felt, be days ahead when he would require every ounce of his newly gained strength. Now he had to build up his reserves for the clash to come. Either Horseshoe would strike soon and suddenly, or else Sugar Loaf would, whoever was ready first and could find the best method to employ for a *coup d'état*.

But Kent hoped and prayed they would be able to get the trail-herd cut out and driven to the loading pens at Sage Junction, some hundred miles north, before Horseshoe tried anything else.

His thoughts turned naturally to Donna. He was worried that she had not been to see him. There was a nagging maggot in his brain and anxiety for her safety and well-being roughened the edges of his nerves, making him moody and sometimes irritable.

Slowly now he turned the sorrel back into the yard, dismounting stiffly, careful about his bound-up ribs.

He trailed the horse's reins and climbed the veranda steps, pulling the rocker forward with the toe of his boot.

He withdrew his makings and rolled and lighted a quirly. It was hard for a man of action to sit around and watch others work. To have to wait, perhaps, for his enemies to storm the gates instead of being able to go out and deal with them first.

He went over in his mind the theory that had been building up inside his brain during the long idle hours which he had endured for the past week.

Although a great deal of it was guesswork, Kent felt sure he had arrived at the solution to the whole mystery.

Mason Hale had wanted Sugar Loaf because, rightly or wrongly, he believed it to be rich in copper deposits. Gus Garner may have told Hale this just to spite him. To dangle the fortune in front of Hale's nose, because Gus hated him, holding him responsible for his son's death.

Shelby was now fairly certain that Garner had been trailed into Three Forks by Chip Bander or one of his men in the belief that Garner was carrying the deeds of his ranch, which indeed he was. Further, Kent believed that they had laid for Garner, only to find the money on him instead of the deeds. Then they had probably hit him and thrown him into Rock Creek.

Mason Hale or Bander, or someone at Horseshoe, had thought fast. They had figured that Garner had sold to Johnnie Montago. It seemed pretty obvious. No doubt they had previously searched the ranch for the title deeds and not finding them had rightly concluded that Garner had them on him.

But instead they had found twenty thousand dollars. That meant, according to Horseshoe's figuring, Garner had sold to Johnnie Montago!

Quite a few folk must have known Johnnie was hoping to buy Sugar Loaf; therefore, he was the natural choice now.

What if Hale had brought in the three outlaws with orders to kill Johnnie, get the deeds off him and take the miners' pay-roll all in the same breath?

That way Hale would hold title to the ranch – and even if it were questioned, possession was nine points of the law – and at the same time swell his reserves considerably with the stolen money!

This theory, Shelby figured, was partly borne out by the fact that the two outlaws they had killed at the line-cabin had three hundred dollars each on them, as though they had been paid for their hold-up by someone higher up. Mason Hale! If they themselves had organized the hold-up it was strange that neither Kent nor Cal had been able to find any trace of the loot in or around the cabin.

Shelby was almost sure they had passed it over to Chip Bander or Mason Hale and had received three hundred dollars each for their part in the business.

Now Horseshoe had tried to scare Kent Shelby and his crew into leaving the spread, even offering to pay for it. Hale was going to get Sugar Loaf, come hell or high water, and Shelby feared they would attack them somehow before Sugar Loaf was ready.

Apart from all this, it was essential to get these beeves to Sage Junction and sell them. He could not afford to wait for a fall trail-drive. Kent needed cash to pay his crew and buy essential supplies.

Three men at least would be needed for the drive. That was little enough to handle even a small herd. But that left only himself to defend the place against a half-dozen or more Horseshoe riders. Tough men, who did not hesitate to kill...

Nearly three hundred cattle were now bunched together less than half a mile from the ranch-house and Shelby had insisted on doing the night-herding himself.

Cal, Charlie and Harry were falling out of their saddles with sheer physical fatigue and lack of sleep. Their faces were bearded and grimed with sweat and dust. White lines of fatigue etched themselves under the eyes and around the stubbled mouths in their otherwise leather-brown faces.

This was a chore Shelby could do, a chance to help in the work at last. He had had his bellyful of sleep and was feeling much stronger now.

Nine days had gone by and still no more from Horseshoe and no word from Donna.

Isobel Montago had been over twice, once with Doc Cleary. She had seen Donna once, in town, with Chip Bander in close attendance.

Harry Busch sat on the darkened veranda, a diminutive form, clutching a heavy-calibre carbine.

'Don't you fret, Mr Shelby,' he said. 'I'm takin' fust watch on the house. Then Cal and Charlie'll split the rest between 'em.'

'You're a good man, Harry,' Shelby said quietly. 'Keep your eyes peeled for trouble. I'm heading out to the herd–'

Both men froze suddenly as the distant drumming of hooves came faintly across the range.

They held still for perhaps the space of three minutes. Then Busch said, 'One rider,

I figger, Mr Shelby.'

Kent nodded slowly. 'You stay here, Harry. Don't wake the others unless you hear shots. I'll handle it.'

'You reckon you kin–' Busch stopped suddenly and blinked. Before he could finish the sentence, Shelby's hand had streaked down and drawn his gun. It was level at his hip the hammer back underneath the strong thumb in the space of a split second.

Kent grinned. 'Don't worry, Harry. I'm not a cripple any more just so long as I don't try riding a sun-fishing bronc.'

He turned and descended the steps into the yard, keeping to the soft shadows cast by the house.

The moon was waning now but it still had power to bathe the range in a silvery light and spotlight the rider now fast approaching the yard.

'Donna!'

'I had to come, Kent,' she called out, 'to warn you. I've been trying to get away for days but Hale's holding me more or less a prisoner. Bander or one of the men's riding herd on me the whole time–'

'Ride along with me, Donna, and tell me what's happened. I'm making for our herd bedded down over yonder.'

'It's about the herd, Kent,' the girl told him breathlessly, 'I–'

'Take it easy, Donna,' Shelby said laying

his hand on her arm. 'Get your breath back first. The news'll keep for a few minutes, I guess.'

'I'm not so sure,' she told him. Her words came more easily now. 'You see, I'm kinda on the run—'

He jerked straight, suddenly, and felt the pain of his injured ribs.

'You mean you're running out on Horseshoe – Mason Hale, or is it that he's given you orders to – drift?'

She shook her head. 'I forfeited the right of any choice when he and Bander found where my sympathies lay. If you're not *for* Horseshoe you must be *against*. All this time I've been a prisoner. Oh, sure, I've been allowed out and about the ranch, even into town, but Bander or someone has ridden close herd on me. I haven't had a chance to get away until tonight and that was only because one of the men, a new hand, risked his job, perhaps even his life, to help me.'

'But what are you aiming to do, Donna? A girl like you cain't just—'

'No! You remember Hale said the west was tough on a girl who was foot-loose! From now on I'm taking my father's name, even if he were a drunkard like Hale claims. I'm Donna Russell now and I'm heading for Sage Junction, Kent. I did find out that we came from there originally. Maybe I can find someone who knew Dad, or maybe even some distant relative. At least I can get some kind of a job there and won't be branded as a – a–'

'We aim to start this herd for Sage Junction day after tomorrow, Donna. You'd better wait here and ride with the boys. It'll be slower but safer.'

'It's about the herd I wanted to see you, Kent,' Donna said as they drew their horses to a standstill and gazed down into the moonlit basin where the dark shapes of cattle made a mosaic pattern on the lighter background of grass.

Shelby rolled a cigarette, watching the cattle with an expert's eye, marking the restless ones as they lumbered to their feet and bawled at the riders and the night, switching tails and moving restlessly round the herd.

Shelby's glance slid down to the girl at his side as a sudden, intuitive idea came to him.

'Horseshoe's getting ready to strike at me through the herd. Is that it, Donna? But how–?'

'You've guessed right, Kent,' Donna Russell replied in her low, husky voice. 'I found out that Hale's had a man watching Sugar Loaf almost day and night. At least I guessed that's' what was happening because from my window I would see a rider come in and hand over glasses to another man ready to ride out. It looks like they've had a roster system working, keeping an eye on Sugar Loaf. They've watched you gather your herd together. I know that now, because last night I was down at the stables, standing quietly in the shadows, trying to figure a way out of all this mess. I overheard Chip and Frank Minden talking. Bill Gunn, I think it was, had just come in to tell them he figured you'd got your herd ready but he reckoned you'd not start your trail-drive until at earliest day after tomorrow. That's Friday isn't it?'

'How did he work that one out, Donna?'

'He told Chip and Frank that he'd been watching over the other side of your range–'

'The north and west sides?'

She nodded. 'South of the copper-mine hills and near to Flying Wagon Wheel's range. Anyway Gunn figured your men must have worked like demons to round up the cattle, brand the strays and cut out a fair trail-herd. He figured they'd have a day's rest before leaving.'

'That means they'll try something Thursday night, Donna.'

'That's the way I see it, Kent. How are you going to be able to fight the whole of Horseshoe, Kent? You'll lose your cattle, maybe your life!'

'I'm not sure, Donna, but forewarned is forearmed. Borden told me that if I wanted help, he'd give it to me with the full backing of the law.'

'But Tom Borden's only one man, Kent–'

133

'He's what law there is around here, Donna. If he and Vern Hanson come out here to back my play, what chance has Chip and his crew to start trouble?'

'I don't know, except that I feel somehow that Borden or Hanson won't stop them.'

Shelby began walking his horse slowly around the herd, the girl keeping abreast of him.

'I've tried to do things the way the law would want them done, Donna,' he said presently. 'I even chanced my arm giving one of the outlaws time to shoot me instead of killing him first–'

'It's all over town, Kent. You've got some friends in Warpath if you only knew.'

'I could use a few friends right now, Donna. Who are they?'

'I heard Brad Straw and Henry Guyler speaking up for you, saying what a disgrace it was that a man should be attacked and almost killed and nothing done by the law about it. Borden was there and he looked mighty uncomfortable.'

'Well that's something to know, Donna. Like I said, I'm trying to follow Borden's advice and play this lawfully instead of resorting to the gun. I'll try it once more. If that doesn't work–' His lips drew together in a thin line and the girl shuddered at what she saw in the blue-grey eyes.

'There's another thing, Donna. If you stay

here, your name'll be dirt. But I cain't let you travel to Sage Junction alone. You'll have to put up with Warpath and the Valley thinking you're a scarlet woman. That's if they ever find out, which I doubt.'

She flushed darkly, but her level green gaze met his oblique glance. 'Do you think I care? I'm quitting the valley. I shall be sorry to leave Isobel. Maybe I can see her once in a while. Apart from that I'll have no regrets, except–'

'Except what, Donna?' His voice was as soft as the night wind.

Her head came up suddenly as she gazed straight ahead across the night-painted range.

'I'll miss you a lot, Kent!'

The morning sun was slanting its rays down from the eastern hills as Warpath rubbed its eyes and took up another day.

Shelby brought the sorrel on to Main, idly watching store and saloon open up and the first of the townsfolk sniff the sage-scented air.

Kent saw Vern Hanson come out of the Chink restaurant and make his way slowly down the board-walk to the sheriff's office.

Henry Guyler came out of his store and his glance laid itself down the stirring street from left to right.

He saw the tall figure on the sorrel and

lifted his hand in salute and waited.

Shelby kneed the horse over to the rack.

'Mornin', Shelby. Glad to see you about again. Anythin' you want from the store. Yore credit's good enough fer me.'

Shelby's gaze swept over the big man. He had only seen him once before, when they had formed the posse on that first memorable Sunday morning. Now this trader was coming forward, making a bold stand in front of the town. He was, Kent Shelby thought, a big man in more senses than one.

He leaned down and proffered his hand and Guyler took it, his long-horn moustache twitching.

'Mebbe you could use some forty-five shells, Kent, or some grub, huh?'

Shelby smiled and slid from leather.

'Lead on, Henry. I could use some tobacco, too.'

Guyler preceded him to the rearmost part of the store. As yet there were no customers.

The storekeeper selected two cigars from an open box on the counter, handed one to Shelby and lit them.

'There's a few of us in town, Kent,' he said puffing clouds of blue smoke, 'who don't take very kindly to Horseshoe's high-handed methods. You kin bet we heerd all about your run-in with Chip Bander and his crew. Some of us felt plumb mad about that, Kent. Brad Straw and Jack Summers, to name just a couple.'

'Thanks, Henry. It's nice to know you've got a few friends when you're bucking a spread like Horseshoe. I've come in to see Borden as a matter of fact.'

'You need help, Kent, you say the word. We ain't fightin' men, we're just ordinary traders, but there's some things as a man cain't stummick.'

Shelby nodded. 'Thanks again. Borden said to come to him if I was in trouble. Well I'm going to do just that. I figure on trailing a small herd up to Sage Junction, but I've got a notion Horseshoe wants to get at the herd first!'

'Could be,' Guyler nodded. 'Jest about what Hale or Bander would figger to do if they wanta bust you up an' send you packin'.'.'

Guyler smiled. 'This valley's covered, Kent. Judge Winter takes care of the town and Mason Hale the range. Looks rather like a partnership though no-one's ever proved it or even said so out loud!'

Shelby considered for a moment. 'Look, Henry,' he said at last, 'you told me just now you'd be willing to help–'

The big man's head nodded emphatically. 'There's a few folks around here, Kent, like I said, who kind of like you and strangely enough dislike Horseshoe.'

'I don't quite know what's going to happen, Henry, but I hope to get my beef herd off by tomorrow, Friday. If all goes well I'll be staying behind on Sugar Loaf. If things don't work out I don't know where I might finish up. In that case could you and Jack Summers and Brad and a few others take it in turns to keep an eye on the place?'

'Be glad to, Kent. Know one or two more men in Warpath who kin be trusted. We could work that all right. You mean see that no-one tries to take over the ranch-house or burn it up?'

'That's what I mean, Henry. I'm going to see Borden now–'

'Reckon he went off to Cottonwood, the county town, by yesterday's stage, now I recollect. Reckon it's Vern Hanson you'll have ter see, Kent.'

Guyler put out a huge, hairy hand and withdrew Shelby's Colt from his gun-belt. He eased back the hammer, ejected a shell and glanced at it.

Without a word he replaced the cartridge and restored the gun to its owner's holster, then the storekeeper reached down under the counter and came up with a box of shells.

'They're for the six-gun, Kent. What's your carbine?'

'Standard Spencer of the Rangers!'

Guyler's thick brows lifted. 'You're not–?'

Shelby grinned. 'No! I'm not a Ranger any longer, Henry. That was years back, but that old ten-shot's as good as a Winchester seventy-three.'

'In the right hands, mebbe,' Guyler grinned, hefting a larger box of shells on to the counter.

'That's the secret,' Kent said. 'Am I good for tobacco, you say?'

Henry Guyler nodded. 'Sure.' He rummaged about on the shelves behind him, fetching out tobacco, papers, flour, sugar, coffee, candles, sulphur matches, a can of coal-oil and a few items of food such as bacon, soda-crackers, etc.

Shelby stared. 'What if I don't make that trail-drive, Henry?'

Guyler leaned forward. 'You'll make it, Kent, I reckon. But even if I thought otherwise it wouldn't make no difference. You standin' up to Horseshoe alone's made one or two of us feel kinda small and mean.'

Chapter IX

Chip Loses a Trick

Vern Hanson moved restlessly in the saddle. 'Reckon I could think of better ways of spending a night, Shelby,' he growled.

'Not if they were your beeves you couldn't,' Shelby replied sharply. 'Reckon we won't have much longer to wait–'

'I ain't so sure,' the deputy said. 'Guess we've only got your word for et thet Horseshoe's out to run off your cattle an' bust you up.'

'You've only got my word for this dressing,' Shelby snapped unbuttoning his shirt to the waist, 'and this gun-sight wound. Maybe you think I tripped over something?'

Harry Busch grinned in the moonlight. 'Reckon me an' Charlie an' Kent can handle this if you got cold feet, Hanson!'

'Who the hell you think you're talkin' to, little man?' Hanson roared, quickly touched to anger at the goading spur of Busch's remark.

Colfax's gaze moved in the direction of the peaceful cattle several hundred yards to their rear. His head cocked to one side. 'Figger I

140

kin hear riders,' he grunted. 'Best keep quiet.'

Shelby's glance flickered over the men much in the way of a commander giving his troops a last-second survey. Harry and Charlie were dependable. That much was certain. Cal was back at the ranch-house ready for anything with his carbine. Unknown to anyone outside was the fact that Donna also was at the Sugar Loaf house. Three men were determined to help Shelby hold his cattle and protect the girl at the same time, come what may. Three men were ready, if needs be, to go down in a hail of lead rather than let Chip Bander and his crew walk over them. The fourth man, Vern Hanson, was an unknown quantity. Shelby sensed that the deputy was uncomfortable. His body was tensed although he denied the likelihood of any action from Horseshoe.

And as they sat quietly listening, the faint drumming of hooves sounded as far away as the twin buttes and Shelby knew that Chip Bander was coming, either to make a try for the cattle, or else to seek out the girl, or both.

The Sugar Loaf men knew what to do. It was all pre-arranged. Shelby's glance lifted to Charlie's face and the oldster turned his horse and melted into the shadow of a clump of thick brush.

'Hey–' Vern Hanson began.

'Easy, Mr Deputy,' Harry Busch said and his voice was a soft, lazy drawl and in his hand was a six-gun that had not been there a second before. For a miner, Harry Busch was right smart adaptable, Kent figured.

They could make out the riders ahead now as they came over a low wash.

Shelby's gaze pin-pointed the high figure of Chip Bander on his blaze-faced bay. Close behind were some four or five riders following Chip Bander's quiet lead.

The Horseshoe ramrod saw them quite suddenly and shocked surprise caused his hands and arms to tighten on the reins, pulling the bay into a walk. For a few moments there was the jingle of bridle-reins and the milling of horses and the half-smothered oaths of men taken by surprise.

The moonlight, as it so happened, glinted on Vern Hanson's badge and Bander's hand came away from his gun with a slow reluctance.

'Howdy, Chip,' Hanson said, and in the brief greeting, Shelby read the deceit and crookedness of the law man.

Whatever Deputy Vern Hanson did he was not going to buck Horseshoe. Such was the protection of the law which Shelby had invoked.

In a way Kent was relieved. He knew now the way things lay and a grim smile touched his lips as he recollected that the Horseshoe bunch were, right now, covered by Charlie's ten-shot carbine!

'Wal,' Bander drawled coolly, 'if it ain't Mr Shelby and – guess I haven't seen this one before!'

'Better look good an' hard now, mister, in case you don't see me agin!' Busch's low-pitched voice matched Bander's drawl.

'I don't get you,' Chip said, puzzled.

'Dead men cain't see, can they?' Busch said softly.

'Why, you–' Bander spluttered and began reaching for his gun.

'Hold it,' Harry Busch snarled and now his voice was no longer a drawl, it snapped like a snaking bull-whip. In his fist was a long-barrelled Colt. It was the fastest draw that anyone there had seen.

Even Vern Hanson blinked and Frank Minden drew back his arm sheepishly, placing both hands on the saddle-horn. Bill Gun, Fish Wilder, Pen Winkler and Ward Reeves sat still, waiting for a lead.

'All right, Bander,' Shelby said coldly. 'You can turn around and go right back the way you came. All of you and make it fast. Hanson! I'm asking you, as the representative of the law to get these men off my land.'

Bander leaned forward in the saddle, addressing Shelby. 'We got a date with some cattle, mister, and ain't nobody round here goin' to stop us. Mebbe your little friend's

143

got a gun out but there's six of us to two of you an' you kin bet Vern won't interfere. Why, he's an old friend of ours–'

'You haven't any date with any cattle, Chip,' Shelby said. 'You had it all figured out to run off my trail-herd. Instead *you're* going to be run off, law or no law. I'm damn' sick of–'

'They ain't doin' any harm on your land, Shelby,' Hanson protested feebly. 'They're only–'

'They're only trespassing,' Shelby rasped, 'and if the law cain't do anything around here but sit on its tail and talk, then there's only one thing to do–'

'And that's this!' Frank Minden snarled, diving for his gun.

Shelby, too, was tensed for action and as Harry Busch's Colt roared in his ear, Kent's hand came up thumping back the hammer of his gun. He threw down on the moving mass in front of him and was faintly surprised to see one man, Ward Reeves, jerk back as he received the full force of the forty-five slug in his chest.

At that moment, Charlie's carbine began its deadly chatter from the brush. Bullets spattered around and a horse squealed and went down. Bander had unwittingly placed himself in a cross-fire and was too anxious to escape the murderous hail of lead to draw his own gun.

They wheeled their horses and the man whose mount had gone down leaped up behind Chip Bander.

Harry Busch levelled his gun again, riding forward and the Colt roared and a man's high-pitched scream tore the night air.

Colfax from the brush had to hold his fire, against that plunging, fast-moving throng of riders. Harry Busch was too far ahead.

Suddenly the whipped riders broke and fled, quirting their horses and fanning out as they raced away. For a matter of seconds they were improbable targets. In a matter of minutes they were gone altogether.

Shelby felt blood trickle down his left arm, for the first time and found where a bullet had grazed his fore-arm. 'That was dam' close,' he thought, and turned to look for the deputy.

Vern Hanson was riding away at an easy gallop, southeast, towards town. Shelby's bitter gaze came back to his own men.

'You all right, Harry, and you, Charlie?'

'Sure.' Both men replied almost together.

'Ride on to the ranch and tell Cal everything's all right so far, Harry,' Shelby said watching the little miner take out at a fast lick.

'Charlie! You watch the herd for an hour or so. We're moving out tonight, instead of tomorrow.'

Colfax nodded. 'You figger they'll try anythin' again, tonight, Kent?'

Shelby shook his head. 'I doubt it, but if you hear anything before we're back, Charlie, you fire three fast shots and we'll be with you.'

'Okay, Kent. Be seein' you. Nice two-timin' bustard, that deputy!'

'That score's not even yet, Charlie. Not by a jugful. We haven't even started yet.'

Colfax grinned and pushed his horse towards the now restless herd. Luckily they hadn't spooked. Even the tough oldster didn't feel like having to cope with a stampede right now.

Donna's face was the whiter, by virtue of the jet-black hair which, loosened from its ribbons, cascaded to her shoulders, forming a dark frame for the pale oval of her face.

She stood for a moment in the doorway of the house, lamp-light limning her with a yellow halation. Then she came forward into the darkness of the porch as Shelby slid stiffly from the saddle and tiredly walked towards the steps.

'Kent!' she whispered. 'Are you all right?'

The very urgency of her anxiety for him sent a warm glow through his body.

'Yes, Donna. We've sent the wolf-pack away to lick their wounds.' He came up on to the veranda and took her by the arms, resisting the impulse to pull her towards him and

146

crush her mouth with his own.

'We're starting the drive in an hour,' he said. 'Can you be ready?'

She laughed, shakily. 'I'm ready now, Kent. Everything I have is packed in a roll behind my saddle.'

'How are you for money?'

She brushed the question aside, leading him into the lamp-lit room.

Harry Busch looked up from cleaning his six-gun and grinned. Cal Eddy came in from the kitchen.

'Cawfee's jest about ready, folks, I–'

'Better fix some sandwiches, Cal,' Shelby said. 'You'll need something to eat in the saddle.'

Eddy nodded but the girl's glance shuttled quickly from Cal to Shelby.

'Do you mean, Kent, that you're–'

Cal said. 'He means, ma'am, that he figgers on stayin' here plumb alone while you ride with me, Charlie and Harry. Me, I don't like it. It was bad enough before you came, beggin' your pardon, Miss Donna.'

Eddy was really worked up.

'You make him come with us, miss. He won't take no notice of me or Charlie. He'll maybe listen to you! Look! What happens when we're well away from here? I'll tell you, Miss Donna. Chip Bander rides in one night with his bunch o' cut-throats an' murderers an' burns this yer place down. Maybe with Kent right here, asleep. I tell you one man cain't fight a hull outfit, not even Kent Shelby and him not fit yet–'

Eddy gazed sheepishly at the three people before him. Busch's dark eyes were bright but he didn't say a thing. Shelby had that mean ornery look that he'd had most times since his beating up. The girl was the only one who would, or could, do anything, Eddy thought as he ambled back to the kitchen.

'Harry,' Kent said. 'Bring Charlie's war-bag along with you. He won't be coming back here. You'll meet him with the herd.'

Busch nodded. 'I'll take care of it, Mr Shelby–'

'For God's sake stop calling me Mr Shelby,' Kent exploded and immediately colour flooded his face. 'I'm sorry. Guess I'm all steamed up.'

Donna's eyes slid to Harry Busch. He let the gun fall back into its holster and stood up.

'Reckon I'll git Charlie's things together,' he muttered and vanished from the room.

She crossed over to Shelby and sat down in the chair next to his.

'All right, Donna. Why don't you say it? What are you waiting for? Tell me what a goddam' fool I am. Tell me that I'm wrong and the men are right–'

His ribs were hurting him again and the little finger on his left hand ached. He knew

148

the scar on his face was white because he could feel the throbbing pain that got into it at such times.

He expected almost anything except the reaction he got. She crossed to the side table on which was a half-empty bottle of whisky and a glass. He watched as she sloshed spirit into the tumbler until it was half full. Then she added a little water from the jug.

'Drink that, Kent,' she said handing him the glass. 'Straight down!'

His glance came up and his eyes softened a little as he saw the imps of mischief dancing at the back of the sea-green eyes.

He took the glass and drank the whisky straight off. Colour stained his face a little and humour came into his eyes.

'You've got quite a way with folks, Donna Russell,' he said.

She watched the old familiar grin spread itself, noticing that the broad lips still bore traces of scars.

'Listen, Kent,' she said earnestly. 'Take that chip off your shoulder. Who the hell cares whether he's right or they're right, or what! If you're set on staying here alone then I'm staying too. Come what may. You wouldn't throw me out. I know that. So you couldn't do anything about it.'

'Are you threatening me?' His mood was half serious, half mocking.

She shook her head. 'No, Kent. I'm not

threatening anyone. I wouldn't do that. We all want you to come. Together we're that much safer, more able to fight back if attacked. Separated we would be playing right into Chip Bander's hands. I know Hale and Bander,' she went on quickly, 'they wouldn't pass up a chance to whittle down this crew. The more you disperse yourselves the better they'll like it. The more you stick together in a bunch, then the less they'll be able to beat you. That was proved tonight out on the range. Harry told me what happened. You three were solid together, Charlie backing you up from the brush—'

'All right, Donna. You don't have to use any more arguments. I'll come quietly, on one condition!'

'What's that?' her voice was sharp with suspicion.

Shelby grinned. 'You do the cooking!'

The task of getting the herd moving at night was rendered less troublesome by the fact that Cal and Charlie had found a big, tough five-year-old steer who was a natural leader.

Once the men had got 'Old Ironsides' on his feet and moving, the others followed, though with a grumbling, bawling reluctance.

Cal and Charlie rode point, Harry and Donna rode the flanks on either side and Shelby, on his own insistence, brought up the rear behind the drag-herd. This was generally the worst position, particularly during the day when the thick yellow dust rose from the twelve hundred cloven hooves, clogging mouth, nostrils and eyes, and settling over the drag riders from hat to boots.

The others saw the reason for Shelby's choice, or the several reasons. Firstly it was often customary for the owner or trail-boss on a cattle-drive to do more if anything of the dirty work than the rest of his crew. Secondly, in Kent Shelby's case, his wounds were such as to preclude any hard, fast riding which might more likely fall to the lot of point and flank riders. Often a steer would get out of line, making a sudden bound away from the main herd. Sometimes it could be got back easily with a few swipes from a coiled *reata*. But sometimes it would bolt and point riders would have to give violent chase and rope it and bring it back before the whole herd started to break the pattern of its movement. The third reason why Shelby had decided to stick in the dust of the drag-herd was in order to keep a sharp eye on their back-trail.

He knew that as soon as Chip Bander discovered they had gone, there was a very good chance of their being followed and attacked. Either openly in daylight with the full weight of Horseshoe and their guns thrown against Sugar Loaf, or else at night, by stealth. Horseshoe might attack a night guard and run off cattle in small numbers or set them stampeding and attack the camp at the same time. There were a hundred ways in which they could ruin Shelby's chances and prevent his getting the herd to Sage Junction.

Constantly, Kent turned in his saddle and gazed backwards across the slowly lightening range. The east was at his back and soon he glimpsed the pearly-grey streaks of approaching dawn. He did not expect to see riders yet but he was not going to be caught unawares. This herd was going to get through whatever the cost!

Along the broad trail they moved slowly but steadily westward. This was the old cattle-trail which divided Sugar Loaf from Flying Wagon Wheel on Sugar Loaf's south-eastern edge.

To the north of the trail were the hills and the copper mines, and later on the trail wound round the base of the hills, turning in a wide arc from west to north, where Sage Junction lay nearly a hundred miles away.

At five o'clock it was broad daylight and without slowing down the herd, the tired crew ate sandwiches and crackers from their saddle-bags. Each rider carried two canteens of fresh water and Shelby led one of the Sugar Loaf ponies, laden with supplies to last them a week. He figured they should make

Sage Junction by the following Thursday or Friday at the latest, thereby averaging about fifteen miles a day. With a comparatively small herd this should not be impossible, although Kent fully realized that any attacks or harassing tactics from Horseshoe later on might well upset the schedule, if nothing worse.

Kent gave another backward glance, slitting his gaze against the sun dead ahead, then he swung the sorrel and his lead-horse away from the drag herd and out of the choking dust, laying his gaze along the right flank of the main herd and watching Donna Russell using her lariat on one or two recalcitrant steers breaking line.

One, indeed, bounded from the main body and Donna touched spurs to her cowpony, bearing down on the dogie at a sharp angle to cut him off and uncoiling the lariat as she went.

Kent, without any knowledge as to her ability in handling cattle, watched with serious interest. He thought out the moves ahead just as though he himself had been chasing the youngster and each time found the girl doing the right thing.

'Goddam,' he thought, 'she's as good as any ranny!'

She had chased the speedy little dogie near to half a mile before being able to close in near enough for a good throw.

In the sharp early morning brightness the men could clearly see what was happening. Dust blew in front of Shelby again and he moved father off the trail away from the milling hooves.

The girl had made her throw and the noose had settled over the horns of the steer. It lowered its head, trying to shake off the rope, but Donna's throw had been too good. It slipped lower and settled round the dogie's neck and immediately the girl made her dally round the saddle-horn and the trained cow-pony dug in its hooves and braced its body for the inevitable pull.

In less than fifteen minutes from the start, Donna had the spirited little dogie back in the herd and glancing up at the watching riders she felt the glow of their approbation. There was a justifiable pride in such a thing, she knew, and did not attempt to deny herelf the pleasurable thrill it gave her. These men had handled cattle all their lives and she had acquitted herself well on the field of battle, as it were!

They grinned and lifted their battered stetsons and from the rear Shelby's arm came up in a salute that seemed to say, 'Good work.'

The herd never broke its stride and dust hung over the valley as the sun rose higher in the slate-blue sky.

They nooned in the saddle and pushed steadily onwards in the blazing heat of the afternoon. Gradually, the sun lowered in the sky and some of the fierceness of the heat subsided. The riders were red-eyed and caked with sweat and dust and Shelby was breathing and eating it, in spite of the bandanna across his face.

Cal Eddy rode up from the front and pulled his horse in alongside the sorrel. He was dirty, unkempt and breathless.

'Bin ridin' ahaid, Kent. Thar's a good place 'bout a mile on to bed down the cattle, jest over the other side of a creek.'

'Good,' Shelby said. 'We can all use a good rest and a meal. Take the pack-horse, Cal, and if you can spare Miss Russell,' Shelby grinned, 'Russell – not Hale – take her along. She can be starting on the meal.'

Cal nodded and took the pack-horse's rein, touching spurs to his mount and riding a wide loop back to reach the girl on the farther side.

Shelby glanced behind and stiffened in the saddle. There was a dust cloud over a distant wash but almost immediately it became obvious that it was a lone rider. It didn't look like Horseshoe would be sending one man.

Kent pulled the sorrel to a halt, letting the cattle drift on. He loosened the Colt in his gun-belt and sat with hands on the saddle-horn, watching and waiting.

Chapter X

Outlawed

At first, Shelby figured the slight figure on the racing pony was that of a girl. For some reason his thoughts flew to Warpath's schoolteacher, Isobel Montago.

Presently, however, he identified the rider as being a youngster of some sixteen or seventeen summers.

The boy's stetson was cuffed up at the front in the vogue set by so many young frontier troopers of the Federal Army. He wore a rough, woollen shirt and turned-up denims, displaying soft leather cow-boots, and his bright, red face was anxious and sweaty.

'You Mr Shelby, Sugar Loaf's boss?' he asked breathlessly, pulling the foam-flecked pony to a dust-raising halt.

Kent nodded and smiled. 'You've sure lathered that horse, son—'

'I had to, mister,' the boy broke in hurriedly 'I'm Terry Guyler, Henry Guyler's son—'

'Henry's son, eh? Well I'm right proud to know you, Terry,' Kent said extending his hand. 'Reckon it was you who took the news to my spread when I was beaten up and Miss Montago helped me. They told me later it was Terry Guyler–'

'That's right, Mr Shelby. But I got wuss news fer you now. Paw found out early today some real bad news. 'Pears like there were some kind o' ruckus out on your spread early last night?'

Kent nodded. 'Chip Bander came in with some of his crew and tried to take my cattle. Vern Hanson was there at my request but he didn't do a durned thing 'cept side with Chip an' then ride away. Reckon we'd best ride on ourselves, Terry, else we'll be losing the herd by night time.'

'Sure, Mr Shelby. Paw said for me to stay with you if I liked. That is – if you'd have me. Gee! I'd shore like–'

'Easy, Terry. Hold your horses,' Kent grinned. 'What's the news?'

'Well, like I was sayin', 'pears there was some shootin' done last night–'

'That's right, Terry. Horseshoe started and we finished it!'

The boy nodded. 'Ward Reeves died, Mr Shelby, and Mason Hale and Chip Bander's got Judge Winter to swear out a warrant for you're arrest.'

'On what charge?' Shelby's eyes were dark.

'Murder, Mr Shelby!" You're outlawed now! They got notices up in town an' they've even stuck one on yore own ranch-house.'

Terry pulled his own bandanna up to his eyes as both men caught up with the dust of the drag-herd.

'What about Tom Borden, Terry, surely he's not–?'

'The sheriff ain't back from Cottonwood, Mr Shelby. That means Vern Hanson an' Judge Winter's got it all their own way.'

'What does your father think, Terry?' Kent asked.

'Paw figgers along with Jack Summers, Brad Straw an' Jim Gil – they all met secretly to talk about it – that it's all a put-up job to get rid of you. Now you're an outlaw with a price on your head anyone can kill you if he can an' be a public hero. Paw figgers even mebbe they sent Tom Borden to Cottonwood a-purpose on some thing or another jest to git him outa the way fer the time bein'–'

'I see,' Shelby said. 'So now Horseshoe can come after me, kill me and my crew and drive back my cattle, all under the protection of Hanson's badge?'

Terry nodded. 'Sure, Mr Shelby, an' Paw figgers mebbe Tom Borden won't even show up again!'

Kent looked at the flushed, eager face of the boy beside him. 'It was a fine thing you did in riding hell-for-breakfast to warn me, Terry. Also it was mighty decent of your dad, but you don't have to join in my battles. You stay overnight at the camp yonder, across the creek and light out early tomorrow.'

Terry Guyler swallowed hard and his glance came up to Shelby's face, straight and unafraid.

'Mr Shelby, Paw says I gotta make my own mind up what to do. He says if I wanta join an outfit and work an' fight for 'em, well I jest gotta, that's all, an' that's how I feel, Mr Shelby. I kin use a gun too and I bin practisin' throwin' a rope. I kin ride – you've seen that. Shucks, sir, I don't wanta go back to Warpath and the store now. Paw understands, he said so.'

They pulled their mounts up at the edge of the creek, watching Harry Busch and Charlie Colfax hazing the steers across after they had drunk deeply. The two riders were in the creek, muddy water reaching to the bellies of the horses and splashing into the men's boots.

'If you're going to draw down a top-hand's pay, Terry, and that isn't much, you'll be expected to do top-hand work. Rope, hog-tie, brand, ear-mark, night-ride, nurse the cattle, guard them and – shoot!'

Terry drew a heavy seventy-seventy Winchester carbine from his saddle boot. 'I won't try it now, Mr Shelby, on account of the cattle, but later on I'll show you I can use this. As to the other things, well I guess

I gotta lot to learn, but I'll work. I'll do all the guard duties–'

'You'll do, Terry,' Shelby smiled. 'But you won't be asked to do more than your share, except in an extreme emergency. If a man were sick or wounded–!'

They put their mounts to the muddy, churned-up water of the creek, crossing to the other side and following the well-beaten trail of the steers until smoke curling up ahead told them that the night-camp was not far away.

Harry Busch was with the herd, bedded down well off the trail, nearly a half-mile away.

Donna's flushed face looked up from the fire over which a pot was suspended emitting savoury smells.

'If it tastes as good as it smells, Donna,' Shelby murmured, 'I'll be fixing to hire you as a cook.'

She laughed. 'Hello, Terry, what brings you here?' and without waiting for an answer spoke to Shelby. 'I might be glad to take you up on that offer!'

'All right, men,' the girl said, 'gather round with plates. Cal, pass me the coffee-pot, will you? Coffee can be heating while you all eat.'

Terry Guyler said. 'If it's all the same to you – er – boss, I'll go down the trail a way and keep a look out. I kin eat presently.'

Kent put a hand on the boy's shoulder. 'You do that, Terry, and thanks for volunteering. Miss Russell 'll keep something hot for you. I'll be down looking for you in an hour.'

The lad climbed into leather and with square, straight-set shoulders, rode out of camp down their back-trail.

When they were through eating, Kent told them of the news that Terry had brought.

Donna's shocked gaze shuttled from one to the other.

'What's going to happen, Kent?'

He shook his head. 'Tom Borden would have been our ace-in-the-hole. He's a sheriff with powers from the county seat. I doubt whether Horseshoe would have gone so far with Tom Borden in Warpath. Unfortunately he's not returned from Cottonwood. Guyler figures maybe someone's holding him there. It might even be worse than that.'

'You mean bushwhacked, Kent?' Colfax said and the other man nodded.

Cal said, 'Looks like we gotta git this herd to Sage Junction an' you gotta git to hell out of it, some place!'

'Where?'

Eddy's gaze lifted to the black silhouette of the copper hills.

'Might be a right smart place to hide out in, Kent,' he said thoughtfully.

'I know those hills like my own back yard,

161

Kent,' Donna said. 'I could take you to a hide-out that no posse would find–'

'I don't know. I'm not figuring on running away.'

'What else kin you do when the cards is stacked against you an' the law's crooked as hell?' Eddy said.

'How can you defend yourselves and look after the herd as well,' Shelby countered, 'just the three of you?'

'Sure, that won't be easy, Kent,' Charlie Colfax grunted, 'but if them bustards, beggin' yore pardon, ma'am, come here an' take you back which is what they'll figger on doin', or shoot you, then I guess we'll be plumb washed up, anyway.'

'It's a hell of a position,' Kent said. 'How far do you figure Mason Hale will go, Donna?'

'For the last week, Kent, he's been as near crazy as makes no difference. He's determined to get rid of you and take over Sugar Loaf and confident that with Vern Hanson and Judge Winter working for him he can square the "law" and if necessary deal with Tom Borden. This I have learned during the last few days!'

Hoof-beats sounded suddenly, close at hand on the trail, and Sugar Loaf backed away from the fire-light into the shadows, and reached for its guns.

The rider came in fast, calling out. 'It's all right, boss, it's me, Terry.'

162

He slid from the pony as Shelby came forward.

'What's up, Terry?'

'They're comin', boss. I bin down the trail a way. Then I figured I'd take a look further on. I know a cut-off that saves four-five miles. Reckon I saw 'em coming, slow and easy like. Recognized Chip Bander and Winkler.'

'How many altogether, Terry?'

The boy considered. 'Couldn't say fer sure, Mr Shelby, but I'd figger all of seven or eight—'

'Listen, Kent,' Donna broke in quickly. 'It's not the cattle they want, right now, it's you. Let me take you into the hills now before they come up. They'll have a job to find us if we can have ten-fifteen minutes start. Then when they've seen you're not here, and go, we can join the herd tomorrow!'

Shelby said. 'They're after us both. I'll have to risk the cattle this time. Terry! The herd's a half-mile away over there. Go tell Harry Busch what's happened and bring him back fast!'

'Okay, boss!' The boy touched spurs to the animal and was away in a flash.

'Listen, Cal and Charlie. Don't on any account make a fight of it. Just tell them you're making the drive alone and you don't know where we are. They won't have been able to follow all our tracks so they won't know how many's in the party. If they make

163

a play for the herd, let them take it. I don't want you boys getting killed for a few steers.'

Donna came up with the horses, saddled and ready.

'We'll play it like you say, Kent. If they don't touch the herd we'll drive on tomorrow. If they do, we'll return to Sugar Loaf. Either way you'll know what's happened when you hit this yer trail tomorrow. We'll be lookin' for you. Good luck!'

'Look after yourselves – and Terry,' Shelby said. 'If anything happens to you I'll personally kill the whole Horseshoe outfit, one by one.'

Donna leaned forward from the neck of her pony and Shelby swung up on to the sorrel.

In a few moments they were lost to sight as the shadows of the hills reached out and submerged them.

Sugar Loaf heard their soft approach and then a rifle's bark shattered the still night and a bullet spanged into the coffee-pot, sending it flying from the fire.

'Any man reaching for a gun is a dead pigeon,' Chip Bander rasped.

'We ain't reachin' fer guns,' Cal Eddy said. 'Our hands is empty!'

'Getting smart at last,' Bander snarled and rode forward into the ring of fire-light.

The three seated men looked up, recognizing Bander, Pen Winkler, Bill Gunn, and Frank Minden wearing a bandage on his hand. The big craggy man in the cut-away coat they sensed was Mason Hale himself.

'We want Kent Shelby and the girl – my girl,' the big man said in a grating voice. 'You men hand them over and there won't be any trouble!'

Eddy was the pre-elected spokesman. 'They ain't ridin' with us on this drive, Mr Hale,' he said politely. 'We ain't seen 'em since we left Sugar Loaf.'

'Why you lying–' Hale's face was roan and mottled in the half-light, anger spilled from him like liquid from an upset vessel.

'Hold et, Mr Hale,' Eddy spoke convincingly. 'We figgered you'd be on our tail pretty soon after what happened last night. It was kinda obvious wasn't it? Sure, Kent wanted to commit suicide an' come along but we done persuaded him not to.'

Bander's cold gaze swung to the other man's face. 'Might be right at that, boss, would be kinda suicide for Shelby to be with his crew right now, though we had to make sure.'

'How do we know they ain't stallin' us, Chip?' Hale snarled. 'Mebbe that dam' bitch is out there in the darkness right now, with Shelby alongside of her! And what's young Guyler doin' here?'

'I–' began Terry, and Colfax cut him short.

'Cal's tellin' this, son,' he gritted.

'Terry wanted to join an outfit an' we was glad to accommodate him on account of Shelby wasn't ridin' with us an' we was plumb short-handed,' Eddy told them with sudden inspiration.

'Sounds reasonable,' Bander said grudgingly. 'I've got a hunch they'll be hidin' out in the hills. Do we bust up the herd, boss?'

Hale pondered for a moment trying to straighten the tangled skein that whisky and anger had made of his thoughts.

He spoke first to Bander, though his glance was red and murderous on Cal Eddy's face. 'Leave the herd for the time being. We'll comb those hills as soon as it's dawn, every dam' inch of 'em. If we don't find what we want, we'll be coming back, Sugar Loaf, and you four men'll sure wish you'd never been born.'

With that, Hale swung his horse around and galloped off into the night, followed closely by his crew.

'We'll stick near by for the night, Chip,' Hale told his ramrod as soon as they were well out of earshot. 'Maybe they're figurin' on comin' back tonight.'

'Won't do any harm to keep an eye on them,' Chip agreed. 'I'll have the boys 'tend to it. Then we can start for the hills as soon as it's light.'

'That was a close shave,' Cal said wiping sweat from his face, 'but I figger we played it right!'

'Ain't never taken so much from any bunch o' gunsels,' Colfax grumbled, 'but I don't reckon we could 'a' done much else.'

'I figgered the bandaged man was goin' for me any time,' Harry Busch said. 'It was my shot as got his hand last night.'

'Lucky for us he didn't, Harry,' Cal grinned.

Harry Busch showed the gun that he had been holding under his coat all the time. 'He'd have gone too,' he said simply and gave his odd smile.

Soon after Shelby and Donna left the camp, the girl oriented herself and after some hesitation struck out in an east-north-easterly direction. It was difficult going at first through the rocky ravines and dry gulches of the foothills. Later, as they climbed higher, narrow trails were more clearly visible, faintly lit as they were by the stars and moonlight.

They waited for a while some two miles from camp, straining their ears for the sound of rifle or six-gun fire. They heard the first shot and Shelby made a move to turn back.

'Wait, Kent,' the girl said. 'If there are no more shots it probably means it was a warning or else someone was reaching for a gun.'

He nodded knowing that if Cal and Charlie and Harry were to have a fight forced on them there would be far more shooting than that. Harry alone, with his lightning draw, would get in three or four shots at least. It looked like Donna was right. Horseshoe had fired a warning shot. There were no other sounds and presently the girl touched his arm.

'We must get on, Kent. They may try to find our trail at dawn.'

'You figure they'll think of looking here?'

She nodded. 'It's the most likely place, but the most difficult. Neither Hale nor Bander know these hills like I do. I used to ride out here as a kid on every possible occasion. If they find us, Kent, it'll be sheer ill luck!'

She led the way on her sure-footed pony, following narrow tracks with no more than a few feet between them and a sheer drop into the rocky ravines below.

Twice they stopped during the night to give the horses a blow and to partake of saddle-rations and water. They refilled canteens at a hill stream and moved on again as the stars paled and slowly winked out.

'We've been veering round to the north-west, haven't we, Donna?' Shelby said presently.

'Yes, for one thing this is rough country and it would be more difficult for them to trail us here. Secondly, we are moving towards the cattle trail that winds around the base of these hills. It will be fairly easy for us to rejoin the outfit when you give the word.'

He noted then that the girl's voice was heavy with fatigue and her body drooped in the saddle. They had ridden all night, all the preceding day and part of the preceding night, and both were just about all in.

Shelby's ribs ached and the cheek-scar throbbed. He still wore the odd-looking nose-patch with which Doc Cleary had contrived to set the broken nose. Kent was only reminded of it now as he wiped the dust and sweat from his face. The nose did not hurt and he thought there was a fair chance that the bones were knitting together in good fashion.

Dawn mists were all about them now, blanketing horse and rider with a thick, wet fog. Kent gathered brush and greasewood and after a time got a fire going in a sheltered rocky spot.

They hunkered down, warming hands and bodies before the welcome blaze, and Shelby unlashed the girl's war-bag and unrolled the two blankets. He unsaddled both horses and hobbled them and placed Donna's saddle under her head and the blankets over her.

'Sleep. I'll wake you later.'

'What about you, Kent?' she mumbled and instantly was fast asleep.

Kent dozed with his carbine at his side, but steadfastly fought off the deep sleep which threatened him.

As the sun rose, the mists thinned and slowly vanished. He found a nearby stream and washed trail fatigue from his face and hands. Then he sought more firewood, returning to the hollowed-out rock and carefully building a fire.

It was the smell of sizzling bacon that finally awoke the girl and Kent grinned. 'Good morning.'

'Breakfast in ten minutes, Donna. There's a stream down there between those rocks if you want to wash up.'

She nodded, rubbing sleep from her eyes and walked down to the bubbling water.

They wolfed down the bacon and dry bread and afterwards Kent rolled a cigarette to smoke with the coffee.

To outward appearances he was relaxed, yet the girl could look closer, and deeper than most. She saw the fires of purpose burning in his eyes and watched the hard edge of impatience ride him as now and again his hand clenched involuntarily and the wound in his face glowed whiter than before.

Suddenly their ears caught the distant sound of hooves striking against rock and shale and Shelby rose, carbine in hand and waited, a greyness enveloping his rigid body.

'Only two riders that I can figure,' he said softly and the girl nodded as she took the six-gun that Shelby proffered.

'You can use it?' he asked and the ghost of a smile touched his broad lips. She nodded and acknowledged his faint humour with an upward curving of her red mouth.

Kent levered a shell into the breech and Donna slowly drew back the hammer of the Colt. It was evident that the riders were coming their way and would see the hobbled mounts if not themselves.

Presently two horses broke through a screen of bushes and came forward along the rocky trail. One horse was being led, the other carried a swaying figure in the saddle. Suddenly the rider stiffened and with a barely suppressed cry put the horses to a trot.

Donna and Kent gaze in shocked amazement at the travel-stained, weary figure of Isobel Montago aboard a paint-pony and leading her own lathered steel-dust!

Chapter XI

Isobel Plays a Hunch

Friday afternoon was a half-day from school and Isobel walked slowly down Warpath's Main Street trying to figure out a list of groceries she would need. She had a notion to ride out to Sugar Loaf later on and take Shelby a home-baked cake or some such small gift. Then she became aware of the prairie-fire gossip around her and her blue eyes travelled slowly over the 'Wanted' notice together with the crudely drawn likeness including the jagged cheek-scar. Kent Shelby! Wanted for the murder of Ward Reeves. She read on, although her mind was not geared to absorb the full significance of the poster's details. She heard folk talking. Something about a trail-drive to Sage Junction and the Sugar Loaf owner not knowing Vern Hanson and Horseshoe were after him.

She gazed around wildly, wondering who she could talk to about this thing. Trying to figure out the more honest traders; those too, who would most likely side with Sugar Loaf. Henry Guyler perhaps or even Brad Straw, or– No! Wait! Jack Summers, the

172

blacksmith. She had overheard him once say it was a pity there were not a few more in the valley like Kent Shelby!

She turned off Main, walking quickly now down to Cross Street, hearing the bellows from the forge and catching glimpses of quick-dying sparks born on the billowing smoke. Jack Summers was still at work and Isobel felt a faint stirring of relief.

His dark-skinned face was shiny wet and his thick brown hair and beard were tangled and sprinkled with tiny fragments of ash.

He wiped his hands on the leather apron and then both face and hands on a rag.

'Afternoon, Miss Montago. Can I help you? Your horse needs a new shoe?'

'Are you alone here, Mr Summers?' she asked, putting her gaze to the man's awesome-looking face. Yet Isobel saw the dark eyes soften with puzzled concern.

'You want help of some kind?'

She came across the shop, giving a wide berth to the anvil. 'What about your fire?'

He smiled broadly. 'Why, Miss Montago, if the fire goes out it can be lit again. Why should I waste time on it when you have come?'

She knew this Jack Summers well enough. She knew that he never minded much what he said. It was the nature of the man to be outspoken. That was why he would speak up for a man like Shelby, who was fighting for

173

his existence against heavy odds. She knew Summers would do what he could to help and she knew also that the blacksmith's brash smile and rolling eyes did not always reflect the true character of the man. In short, Isobel Montago knew that if indeed there were a gentleman in Warpath then that one was big, bearded, sweaty Jack Summers.

'Listen, Mr Summers,' the girl said softly. 'I've just seen the "Wanted" notices. Dodgers pinned all over the town for Kent Shelby. I came to you because, well, because–'

His bright glance slanted down on the girl's upturned face. 'Because you think I might be a friend of this Kent Shelby?'

She swallowed hard and dropped her gaze. Then her eyes came up, blue, challenging, unafraid. 'Yes, Mr Summers. I guess that's about it. It appears to me Mr Shelby's badly in need of friends.'

He pointed to a chair and quickly wiped it over for her with his rag. Then he picked up a pipe and lit it, putting his glance through the blue wreaths of smoke.

'All right, little girl, I'll tell you. I don't know this Shelby much. Guess I've only seen him once apart from when he first came here and killed an outlaw as cool as all get-out. But what I know about him I like. I know he's bucked Chip Bander an' Mason Hale. Even heard he told Vern Hanson a thing or two, though I reckon I'm wastin' time with all this, seein' how it was you helped save his life.'

She inclined her head. 'He's too good a man to die, Jack – Mr Summers! Why should these killers be allowed to drive a man from his own place, murder him, even?'

Summers eyes twinkled. 'You kin go right on calling me, Jack,' he said. 'I like it, though I can see the way the wind's blowing.'

He crossed over to the girl and laid a beefy hand on her shoulder.

'What you figger on doin', Miss Montago?'

She looked up and Summers was struck by the force of her resolve clearly etched on her face and in her blue eyes.

'I've got to get to him, Jack, and warn him that Vern Hanson's after his blood–'

'Judge Winter too,' Summers put in, 'and the whole of Horseshoe tryin' to make the thing appear legal.'

'Anything else you know, Jack?'

He thought for a moment. 'Guess I almost forgot one of the most important things. All this could only've happened without Tom Borden being here. He took the stage to Cottonwood Wednesday. He's not back. It doesn't look so good.'

'I see. You mean you think Hanson or Winter or someone's had him – detained or something, to keep him out of the way?'

'Reckon it's more than likely. Tom figured on being back here Thursday night. Hanson's

175

shore moved fast.'

'What about this trail-drive, Jack? Do you figure Shelby would have gone?'

Summers dropped his voice. 'Henry Guyler had a look at Sugar Loaf this morning. We kind of agreed with Shelby to keep an eye on the place although he had told Guyler he wasn't going on the drive. That's as maybe. Henry had a good look round. The place was deserted and Shelby's sorrel was gone from the stable!'

'What's your guess, Jack?'

Summers lifted his hips to the anvil and with complete unconcern, watched the fire die down.

'You probably don't know, Miss Montago, that Donna Hale's run out on Horseshoe. They tried to keep it quiet, but it wasn't no use. Seems like Hale and her had a bust-up–'

'On account of the persecution of Sugar Loaf?'

Summers's eyes widened. 'Say, that's about it, I'd figger! Anyway Hale and Chip Bander are out to nail Donna's hide as well as Shelby's.'

'Tell me, Jack,' she asked again. 'What's your guess about Shelby?'

'Let's try the process of elimination, Isobel,' Summers suggested. 'First, Shelby could have stayed on at the ranch. He doesn't appear to have done that, though of

176

course he might be hiding out some place close by. Second, he could have gone with his crew, hoping to fight off Horseshoe when they catch up with him. Third, he could take to the hills, but I guess he doesn't know the trails–'

'Wait!' Isobel jumped up from the chair and caught hold of the blacksmith's arm excitedly.

'Shelby doesn't know the hill trails, that's true – he's a stranger. But Donna Hale knows them blindfolded!'

Summers felt his pulse quicken almost imperceptibly. He gazed long and hard at the girl's eager, flushed face.

'You might have it, Isobel,' he said at last, breathing deeply. 'You might have it!'

'I'm taking my steel-dust, Jack, tonight. Can you help me get out of town unobserved?'

He grinned. 'That's an easy one, but you sure you know what you're doing? Supposing Shelby's with his trail crew, after all?'

'I'll take care of that, Jack. I've got a strong feeling about all this.'

'Look, Isobel,' Summers said. 'You want for me to come along?'

She shook her head and smiled. 'I know exactly what I'm going to do, Jack, but thank you.' She held out her gloved hand and Summers took it gently in his own massive paw.

'All right, if that's how you want it, but you've got two horses, haven't you?'

She nodded, mystified.

'You saddle 'em both up and fix to have canteens on the saddle. You'll need two horses if you're going to ride fast across the valley to the hills. Now, this is what you do tonight...'

Warpath's mood tonight was different, subtly different. There was a thin, razor-edged atmosphere of expectancy that, for all its fineness, was felt sharply enough by some.

Jack Summers heard the whisper of impending things in the evening breeze as it stirred the dust outside the shop.

Henry Guyler's senses were sharpened acutely to the town's different beat. True, Henry Guyler was thinking of his son Terry, and what the separation would mean to them both. Yet, if Shelby could stage a comeback, there need be no going away, as such, for Terry. They would see each other often enough. Only if Shelby and his small band of loyal followers failed, only then would Henry Guyler's parting with his son be well-nigh unbearable in its tragic sequence. For if Shelby failed and Horseshoe triumphed, there would be no man of Sugar Loaf left alive, and Henry Guyler swore an oath that Hale and his crew would dangle from the highest tree, whatever mockery Vern Hanson made of the law.

Brad Straw of the saddlery would be going down to Sugar Loaf presently and the bean-pole man, too, felt the unnatural beat and whispered temper of the town, even above the usual raucous shouting and singing from the saloons and dance halls.

Brad felt with Jack and Henry and Jim Gil, the liveryman, that something would soon have to be done about this hard, brash crew. When Chip Bander and his men came to town every Saturday night they often as not tore it wide apart. The sky was the limit and when they had gone, honest traders stared at their broken store windows and started in counting the cost. Sometimes the cost was even higher than damaged property. It was getting so it wasn't safe for a woman to be on the streets when Horseshoe was in town.

The piano from the Last Frontier tinkled out across the light-slashed board-walk and Vern Hanson, leaning against the door-jamb of the sheriff's office across the way, felt his nerves tighten at the strident voices of the percentage girls.

The Grand Hotel was a little quieter, more select. But the street was noisier than usual for a week-night. Drovers came in, miners, cowboys from Pothook and Flying Wagon Wheel, and a few freight wagons on their way farther west.

Yet above all the discordant noise and

movement out front, Vern Hanson also heard the whispering voice of a town that was tired of being pushed too far for too long.

'Maybe,' he thought, with rare insight, 'it's my own pulse-beat I can hear, or the still and small voice of conscience.'

This time, Vern Hanson's lean, saddle-leather face actually creased into a grin as his bright glance idly moved over the traffic on the street. He didn't kid himself about that conscience. The question of two-timing Chip Bander and Horseshoe had nothing to do with morals.

Vern eased himself slightly, shifting his weight and hooking thumbs into his belt. He knew the chance he would be taking but he also knew that his usefulness to Mason Hale was almost through. Chip Bander had told him in as many words, this very day!

'Listen, Vern,' Bander had said and his face was even more ugly and cold when he smiled. 'Don't you worry none about Shelby. Horseshoe'll take care of him.'

'Reckon I should come along with you as a law officer, Chip,' Hanson had said and had felt Bander's cold gaze bore into him.

'You don't have to worry figgerin' things out, Vern,' he had replied. 'You just stick to doin' what you're told, see?'

Then it was that Vern, not an over-imaginative man, had felt the first stirrings of trouble; had seen the faint glimmerings of a red light ahead.

'What about Borden?' Hanson had said.

Chip had half turned away and then come back, putting a large hand on Hanson's chest and pushing gently, suggestively, so that the deputy was rocked back on his heels.

'You keep Borden tied up where he is. Where he cain't do any harm. When the time comes, we'll tell you!'

Hanson now rolled a cigarette, mechanically nodding as men greeted him in the light spilling from the office at back.

A roughness broke over his face, coinciding with the light from the spluttering sulphur match and sponging away the faint bitterness, the hurt pride that had been there in the darkness a moment before.

It was as though the hard core of his resolve had exploded with the match at one and the same time. He watched Guyler come on to the side-walk, pause for a second, and move down-street towards the livery. Yet Vern waited and stood there, feeling the need for a drink as a rising urgency in his belly and throat.

He saw Brad Straw cross through the dust of Main, threading a leisurely way betwixt moving traffic, and later still Summers walked idly by in the same direction.

Without fully understanding these things or their significance, Vern felt their impact, slight and distant as it was.

Intuitively he sensed the time would soon be ripe to move. The time when he would recross the trail back from crookedness to law and order. He had his hand on the lever and savoured the thought as he smoked his cigarette. His was the power which could upset Hale's and Bander's plans, and all he had to do was to saddle quietly and move out to the deserted stage-station on the west trail where Sheriff Tom Borden lay bound and gagged!

It was about nine o'clock, or a little after, when Vern Hanson's glance had reached through the darkness to pinpoint Jack Summers as he passed in front of a lighted doorway.

The blacksmith had just seen Isobel Montago on her way. She had been aboard the steel-dust, leading the second pony on a long rein. She had met Jack Summers, as arranged, in a vacant plot inhabited only by derelict cabins and rising weeds and grass.

He had seen to it that the girl was well equipped. A six-gun with ammunition, food in her saddle-bags, whisky, water and bandages. He had inspected the shoes on the two horses and proclaimed them good enough for the chore ahead.

Now, well away from town, the schoolteacher set the steel-dust to the valley and once there she put both horses to a steady, mile-eating run.

At ten she stopped to breathe the horses, and again at eleven and midnight. Her pocket-watch pointed to one o'clock when she brushed the low foothills.

She was cold and glad of some of the food she had packed. She even tried some of the whisky, nearly choking, but feeling wonderfully invigorated and warmer.

Later, she quenched her thirst with water from one of the canteens and suddenly wondered just how she was going to begin so vast a task as the one she had planned for herself.

She put her gaze to the forbidding copper hills, dark and mysterious, against the starlit sky. Her mind groped for a way even as her eyes sought a path.

She tried to remember the various inlets to the hills as she had seen them in daylight and walked her horse slowly round the lower slopes and boulders and almost came smack bang into a camp a hundred yards ahead!

She saw the fire now and the black shapes of men, and slowly, painfully turned the horses, praying that neither they nor the other mounts would nicker; praying that her own horses would not strike a sharp rock or stone on the loose earth.

Those next ten minutes were just about the worst she had ever experienced except when she thought back on the Sunday morning and later when she had helped Shelby after Horseshoe's brutal attack.

Each second, as she reviewed these things in her mind, she expected to hear the shouts of roused men and feel a bullet tear into her back.

But by the grace of God she made it back whence she had come and stood still with the horses, listening to the sounds of the night and the trip-hammer beating of her own heart.

Suddenly an idea came to her and she shuddered at the very thought of it. Yet she knew, even as she tremblingly dismounted, that she would do this thing, come what may.

If she could creep up on this camp and discover who or what they were, she might perhaps hear something that would give her a lead.

Whilst her mind told her other things, her pounding and shaking limbs told her that the men ahead were Horseshoe.

Now Isobel tied the horses to a clump of thick brush, not daring to risk leaving them with trailing reins.

Quietly, breathlessly she crept forward, yard by yard, foot by foot, taking advantage of every possible shadow and piece of cover.

At last she dropped to the ground and began snaking forward, nearer and nearer to the circle of men. The voices came clearly now and words began to form and make sense to the listening girl.

She saw at once by the blanketed forms that some men were asleep. But two figures sat talking and with a rush of breath to her throat she recognized the huge bulk of Mason Hale, at the same time identifying his voice.

'Doesn't look much like they're joining up with the outfit tonight, Chip,' Hale growled. 'Supposin' they aren't even in the hills?'

'Donna knows them hills, boss. Seems like she would figger it a natural hide-out for her an' Shelby. Anyway, we'll soon see come sun-up. We're bound to cut their sign some place leadin' from the cattle tracks. If we don't, we'll know they ain't here at all. Reckon we kin git some sleep. The boys'll warn us soon enough if anything happens.'

Isobel held her breath and inched her way slowly backward, not daring to turn until she was out of ear-shot of the camp. She stood by the horses, thinking; realizing that Horseshoe had figured as she had done. Namely that Donna had taken Shelby into the hills, either because they had already had a brush with Horseshoe or else because they had discovered Horseshoe's presence.

It looked as though her hunch or her reasoning were at least as good as Mason Hale's and Chip Bander's. They were going to wait until dawn and then try to track the two people they had reason to believe had fled to the hills. If they ever caught up with them—! Isobel shuddered. Two more murders would smear and stain this valley with the blood of dark violence.

She mounted the paint pony now, noticing that the steel-dust was lathered and tired. Soon she was climbing the ascending trails, relying purely on instinct and luck to point her the right way.

She must find Shelby and the girl before Horseshoe discovered them!

Chapter XII

'I'm Going Back to Warpath'

Even for a range-bred girl it had not been a pleasant way to spend a night. Not in the hills. Now the cold dawn mists were thinning and the sun was coming through with heat enough to warm chilled bones.

Isobel took a pull from the whisky flask and felt better, almost light-headed, and as her glance dropped to the ground she saw the scuffed earth and tufts of pressed-down grass left by the recent passage of one or two horses.

She was no sign-reader, but she had a woman's sixth sense which served her in good stead.

She pushed the horse up the slope, plunging through a thicket and coming out on to a stony, ascending trail.

Her glance went ahead and took in the grim-faced figure ahead, holding the carbine, and the girl next to him with the cocked revolver in her hand.

A choking cry, half hysterical, escaped from Isobel's throat as she put the horses forward and clattered to meet them. She had won! her heart sang. She had beaten Horseshoe!

Donna Russell brushed a hand across her face in an instinctive gesture. Then she slowly let go the hammer of the six-gun and thrust the Colt into the waistband of her skirt. She stepped forward, arms outstretched, and Isobel half fell from the saddle, sobbing a little because near-hysteria was quickly giving place to joy.

'You look about all in, Isobel,' Shelby smiled. He indicated the hide-out between the rocks. 'Come into the camp and tell us what's been happening! Here, let me take the horses.'

Donna put an arm around the girl and led her through the concealing brush and protecting rock to their camp.

'You need something to eat, Isobel,' Donna Russell said, putting bacon and beans into the skillet and placing it over the fire.

'There isn't time, Donna,' the school-teacher said as calmly as possible.

'Kent! I came here to warn you, to tell you that you've been proclaimed an outlaw and that Horseshoe is on your trail right now, probably–'

'You give me the story while you eat, Isobel,' Shelby said coolly. 'I'll keep an ear open and so will the sorrel. We'll have the fire out too, soon as that food's cooked!'

Nevertheless, Shelby laid the carbine close

by his hand after pulling the horses well back behind the rocks.

He rolled and lit a cigarette as he sat listening to the girl's story.

'Your facts, together with your hunches, pretty well add up to the correct total,' Kent said presently, 'although it now appears that Horseshoe's around some place. I'd figured they had gone back to their spread.'

Shelby rose suddenly to his feet. 'We'll have to join the herd before it's too late, Donna. What are you figuring on doing, Isobel, maybe you'd better come–'

'It's too late now, I think,' Isobel Montago exclaimed as two horses nickered and the sound of hoof-beats came to their ears.

'Sounds like one rider only,' Kent said, 'but there may be others about. Get on your horses!'

They climbed aboard and drew out of the camp, in order to take to the rougher, brush-protected country.

There was a rider not more than fifty yards away and Shelby saw through a red mist the high figure of Chip Bander atop the blaze-faced bay! Bander, who, unknown to anyone had come across Isobel's tracks and followed them – here!

'Get back behind the rocks!' Shelby yelled and drew his carbine, realizing that he would have to use the Spencer because Donna had his six-gun.

189

Bander's face was a cold mask of evil as he drew his Colt and fired, but Shelby's carbine shot came first. It was too hurried to have found its target. Instead, the sudden, sharp bark of the carbine had caused Isobel's paint to rear and then rush forward.

Bander, half in range half in panic, perhaps, as he glimpsed the spirited horse charging down on him, levelled and fired his gun. Three rapid shots, sounding almost like one, roared out and from the corner of his eye Shelby glimpsed the schoolteacher sway and fall from the back of the now veering horse.

A terrible fury swept over Shelby as the significance of what had happened sank into his brain.

Bander's crimes had been bad enough before and Shelby had promised a settlement. Now the greatest crime of all had been enacted before his very eyes. Greater even than cattle or horse stealing. Woman shooting!

Forgetful of his hurts, Kent rowelled the sorrel from a standstill to a racing gallop, setting the plunging horse on a dead-straight course for the Horseshoe ramrod, firing the carbine as he went.

Chip Bander brought the barrel of the Colt down and fired point-blank at the charging figure ahead and cursed obscenely as the hammer fell on a spent shell. He swung the gun and threw it wildly at Kent's head as Shelby's last carbine shot caught the bay horse and sent it down.

The gun grazed Shelby's forehead, momentarily spinning his senses. He gazed down at the sprawled figure of the Horseshoe ramrod, suddenly shocked as Bander produced another gun from somewhere and triggered lead upwards in a burst of insane violence.

A bullet scorched the sorrel's neck and the horse screamed and reared up, forelegs thrashing the air inches from the half-sprawled, half-crouched figure on the ground.

A red mist came down over Kent Shelby's eyes as he let the sorrel have its head and Bander screamed.

There was a part of him, a small part that whispered that this thing was wrong, and then recollection of Chip Bander's unutterable evil flooded back and the sorrel's shod feet pounded bone and flesh into a bloody, shapeless and unrecognizable mass...

Donna was kneeling by the fallen girl, pillowing Isobel's head in her lap. Shelby watched the sun glinting on the red-coppery tresses, too numb to think, too angry to feel anything except the riding fury of the moment.

'If any of the crew are around, Kent, they'll have heard those shots and will come running!'

He shook himself as the import of the

girl's words penetrated his armour of bitter wrath. He rode the sorrel back, dismounted and picked up Bander's other gun. It was undamaged and so were a few of the forty-five shells in the dead ramrod's belt.

Shelby bent down and loaded the six-gun, thrusting it into the holster at his hip. Bander's horse, he found, was dead. The sooner they were away from here the better!

He led the sorrel back to where Donna knelt.

'Have you whisky?' she asked.

'You mean she's not–?'

'I'm not certain, Kent. It's touch and go.'

Shelby produced a whisky flask from his saddle-bag and handed it to Donna Russell, watching her with his eyes but wondering what the rest of Horseshoe were about and if they were near, and whether there was a chance for himself and Donna with a dying woman on their hands.

Donna worked hard to stop the frightening loss of blood and Kent felt suddenly sick of the smell of gun-smoke and blood and death. There was something more to it than that, he knew. It was as though he had been beating his brains out against a wall and had suddenly stopped, realizing the futility of it. Realizing the hurt it was doing to others as well as himself.

It was one thing for a man to fight for his own things and get hurt. It was something else if innocent people became involved. Isobel had done a great deal, Shelby thought. She had taken a big risk, had gambled and had lost. Or as near lost as made no nevermind.

'Donna,' he said quietly. 'I'm going back to Warparth.'

She raised a tear-stained face, now made rigid by his words.

'Kent! You cain't–' She stopped abruptly, halted by the burning light in his dark gaze.

'I must take her back, Donna. She must have a doctor. Maybe there's a chance, a slim one, but–'

'They'll take you, Kent,' Donna said tonelessly.

'I must chance it. I must chance running into them on the way back. So far it looks like Chip was scouting away from the others. You join up with the herd, Donna. Tell Cal and Eddy to push on for Sage Junction for all their worth. I'll join them later, maybe.'

He stooped and gathered the unconscious girl in his arms, holding the slack body across the saddle whilst he carefully mounted.

Donna turned to her pony. 'I'll take the steel-dust, Kent. You may have need of the paint.'

He nodded sombrely and sought directions from the girl. 'Good luck, Donna,' he said and turned the sorrel in the direction she had indicated.

She answered softly, but so softly he did not hear and was unaware that he had not heard her reply.

She watched him astride the sorrel with the wounded girl in his arms and leading the paint, and thought she knew why he was going back.

With a scarcely suppressed sob, Donna Russell neck-reined her mount and plunged down into the brush- and rock-covered gullies of the lower hills.

Vern Hanson moved at last. Not to the Grand Hotel but down to the Last Frontier saloon where he as less likely to meet his immediate friends.

The long-legged rangy buckskin at the hitch-rack was Vern's own and now, unobtrusively, he slid into the hull and leisured the horse down towards the red-light district. The Last Frontier was half-way down, standing on an invisible line separating respectability from sin!

The drink had been worth waiting for, Hanson considered as he slowly sipped the rye and water and let his mind dwell on the prospects ahead.

Firstly it was obvious from Horseshoe's attitude that they no longer considered Vern Hanson worth his money. True, Bander had paid him extra only the other day. Surprising, it was, considering that Vern hadn't expected it. But Chip Bander had added his cheap sneers and barely concealed insults and Vern had at last glimpsed the writing on the wall!

God! It was a lucky thing that he and the two hired thugs had been able to snatch Borden from the stage-coach before either the sheriff or Froom Lester, the driver, had gotten a glimpse of them! They had been well masked and Vern had worn old clothes that had not seen the light of day for many a year. The men's hats had been well pulled down over their eyes and there had been nothing by which Borden or Froom or anyone could have identified them.

In any case, Zeller and Pim had drifted on, as arranged, well satisfied with their easy fifty dollars apiece. Now all Vern had to do was to cook up a convincing little story and release the helpless sheriff.

Once Borden was back in Warpath the sparks would fly. Vern grinned. Tom Borden might be slow to move at first, but after this there would be no stopping him!

With the two whiskies under his belt, the deputy resisted the temptation to stay for more. It was a long ride to Sand Flats stage station, and besides, he had a half-pint bottle in his saddle-pockets!

He took the west trail and as he rode his eyes lifted to the north-west where the copper-hills lay dark against the night sky.

He wondered what sort of luck Chip Bander and the boys were having and suddenly considered a possibility that until this moment had not occurred to him. It would be a hell of a thing, he thought, grinning, if this Kent Shelby outsmarted Mason Hale and his Horseshoe outfit. If such a thing could possibly happen then he, Vern, would undoubtedly be on the right side of the fence. But if, as was probable, Horseshoe rode over Sugar Loaf and smashed it, then Vern would have to go very carefully. Maybe his law badge and Tom Borden's big body would not be sufficient protection.

Still, there was a way to play this if a man was right smart careful...

Shortly after midnight, Hanson pulled up by the side of the trail and sampled some whisky. His gaze swept the starry heavens without even seeing the jewelled magnificence of the dark indigo sky. His eye was to the moon, quartering towards the southwest, and he watched it and gauged the time as accurately as reading a clock.

The sky and the moon and sun and stars were his landmarks, his compass points. Nothing else. They held no splendour or beauty. Vern Hanson would have been mildly surprised if anyone had ever suggested such a thing.

Similarly the trembling aspen trees on the higher levels, the outspreading cotton-

196

woods, the clumps of chaparral, the patches of wild flowers, all these things were points by which a man oriented himself. What else?

Thus, Vern Hanson knew the range from one point of view only. He could set his course and say, 'I will be there in five hours' time when the moon is dipping over that distant smudge of trees.'

An almost imperceptible lessening of the intense darkness in the eastern sky was sufficient to tell Vern Hanson that dawn was not much more than an hour away.

He gazed now at the derelict stage station, a 'dobe building that at one time had offered Express mail riders a change of horse and a hastily consumed drink. Later when the overland stage had started its regular schedule, using the cut-off which saved about three miles on the way to San Veronica, the station had 'jest natcherally fallen plum apart,' in the words of an oldster stage driver.

That was not strictly true as, though the corrals had partly collapsed, the 'dobe building itself was as good as ever. The driver had been referring more to the place as a social centre where a man could always have a chat with Bart Schliecher and perhaps exchange gossip with a U.S. mail-rider. Now the people had gone and in that respect the place had 'fallen plumb apart.'

The deputy dismounted and struck a match to the wick of the coal-oil hurricane lamp he had brought for a specific purpose. He began talking to himself, knowing that his voice would carry to the mud building. Vern Hanson's act had begun. His boots crunched on stones and debris and occasionally kicked at a rusty can, a relic of Bart Schliecher's days.

He heard a faint noise now and grinned, almost with relief. Vern had seen to it that food and water had been left within reach and the gag had been a mere formality. In any case Borden could have shouted himself hoarse. No one would hear him except perhaps a wandering party of Indians.

Still, Hanson was relieved. Even with food and water within reach, things could happen to a man tied up for two or three days miles from anywhere.

Vern held the lantern in his left hand. In his right was a gleaming Colt. Bravely, fearlessly he crossed the threshold and glimpsed the half-tied figure of Sheriff Tom Borden.

The gag was down around his chin as might have been expected, but Hanson was forced to admit that Borden had made a good job in getting half-free of the ropes. They had very nearly tied him too securely.

Tom's eyes narrowed and for a moment all he saw was the gun in Hanson's hand. Then he recognised his deputy and a long-drawn cry of relief escaped his lips.

'Thank the Lord I found you, Tom,'

Hanson said, producing what was left of the whisky. 'Here, take a pull at this. How long you bin tied up like this? Not since–?'

Borden shook his head, feeling the beginnings of strength trickle back into his body. Hanson cut the ropes away, but for a long time Borden could not move his legs.

'Some bustards jumped me on my way back from Cottonwood, Vern. Don't even know where the hell I am. Bin here quite long enough though. Goddam glad they left me a bit o' food an' water.'

'Reckon it's all to do with the trouble going on in the valley, Tom,' Hanson told him. 'Horsehoe's got plumb out of hand an' I figger Chip Bander an' Mason Hale's pretty near crazy. They've got Judge Winter to swear out a warrant for Kent Shelby. They forced me at the point of the gun to pin up notices.'

'Godamighty,' Borden said at last, struggling to rise to his feet. 'What have we got, mob rule?'

'Ain't much better as I kin see it, Tom. Town's gittin' mighty restless. Jack Summers, Henry Guyler, Brad Straw, Jim Gil, to name a few.'

'How did you find me, Vern, and where are we anyway?'

'This here's the old stage station some four miles off the stage road. Remember? As to how I found you, Tom, well I kinda hoped

I might pick up some sorta lead if I came out on the stage route to Cottonwood. I bin wanderin' about all night. Then I suddenly thought of this place an' took a *pasear* over. I heard someone cry out, so I lit the lamp an' came in with a gun not knowin' quite what I'd find.'

Tom Borden gripped the other's arm. 'I'll never be able to thank you enough for this, Vern. You got a drop more whisky to spare?'

The deputy nodded and handed Borden the bottle. He took some and passed it back. Vern drained the bottle and slung it outside in the trash heap.

'What horse you got, Vern? Can it carry double?'

Hanson grinned. 'Lucky I brought the buckskin. If we take it slow and easy we kin git back before noon.'

'Let's go,' Tom Borden said, and there was a bright gleam in his eye which owed nothing to the golden halation now showing in the east.

Chapter XIII

Stirrings Beneath the Surface

Without Donna's guidance and knowledge of the trails, Kent Shelby found the journey back a hellish chore. Apart from sometimes having to retrace his steps when a trail petered out to choked brush or the edge of a steep ravine, apart from this, there was the ever constant chance of meeting up with the rest of Horseshoe. To this end, Shelby's right fist held Chip Bander's fully loaded Colt.

There were six loads in the gun, ready and waiting for Horseshoe if they should cross his trail and such was Shelby's cold rage that he softly prayed for a chance of meeting with Bander's crew of gunsels.

Those six bullets were going to tell, he promised grimly, whatever the cost to himself. And such is the capricious way of Fate, that Kent Shelby's sorrel travelled all morning with a double load through the hills with nary a sign or smell of another Horseshoe rider!

How it was that Chip had become separated from the others, Kent did not even try to guess. Perhaps he had deliberately under-taken to 'beat' that section of hills on his own. Perhaps he had done this as a result of a hunch, or maybe he had unwittingly strayed from the trail or followed tracks on his own initiative. It didn't much matter. However it had happened it had been a mis-take from Chip Bander's point of view.

One or two backward glances had served to show Kent that the buzzards were already wheeling high in the sky above that section of the hills. If a coyote or timber wolf didn't get there first, the buzzards would soon swoop down and begin their obscene business.

Once, from the top of a jagged rise, Shelby glimpsed the coppermine workings, near to the main cattle trail in the lower hills, and the sight momentarily brought his thoughts to the question of copper under Sugar Loaf land.

That problem would have to wait until the fight with Horseshoe was settled, once and for all, and Kent did not rate his own chances very high. He figured there were still probably a half-dozen or so hands without Ward Reeves and Chip Bander. Hale would have murder in his heart and sooner or later would discover that neither he nor Donna was in the hills.

News would travel over the 'prairie telegraph' and Mason Hale would come to town with his crew at his back, for the final reckoning with Shelby. Once Shelby was out of the way, then Hale could deal with the others easily.

Without placing too great an importance on himself, Kent considered this was the way Hale would figure things. And soon now Kent would be proved right in his reasoning.

He glanced down again at the ashen face of the girl as she momentarily stirred in his arms. Once during the ride he had forced a trickle of spirit between her teeth. A lot had spilled but some had gone down. Enough to help her a little.

He began wondering what he would do if Isobel died before things were settled. A law-abiding man did not take a gun and seek out a whole outfit and shoot them down, and yet, Kent thought grimly, 'I am no longer a law-abiding man. There is precious little law by which to abide!'

If Vern Hanson were on Horseshoe's payroll and Judge Winter as well, how could Tom Borden hope to fight that kind of opposition, even supposing he had a mind to?

He came into Warpath when the town was drowsing in the furnace-heat of the afternoon. He was tired, and alkali dust covered his sweat-stained face in a greyish-white mask.

The town stirred, blinked and rubbed its

eyes and arose as the mounted man on the dust-caked sorrel slowly rode down Main towards Doc Cleary's cottage.

Men and women came out on the side-walk and laid their shocked gazes on the white-faced girl in Kent Shelby's arms.

He had to halt the sorrel as the crowd spilled from the board-walk, and then broke as Sheriff Tom Borden came striding through, followed by his chief deputy.

Shelby waited until the barrage of questions had been fired and then his bleak gaze slanted down on Borden's face.

'Glad you're back, Tom,' he said and Borden wondered at the man's wooden face, the smouldering eyes and the dead-level monotone of his voice.

'Horseshoe jumped my outfit again,' Shelby went on and smiled without humour. 'It's getting monotonous. Donna was with us and we two lit out for the hills—'

He moved the girl gently in his arms and said, 'Goddam it, the story can wait. Maybe Doc Cleary can save her yet!'

He kneed the sorrel forward and the crowd broke away.

Jack Summers stood on the board-walk, his dark glance taking in the picture out front. He, alone of the townsfolk, could guess what had happened and his eyes met Guyler's intent gaze and Summers moved his head so that Guyler nodded and began walking towards him…

Doc Cleary straightened up and looked at the three men before him.

'What's the verdict, Doc?' Tom Borden asked. The same question lay in the eyes of Shelby and Vern Hanson.

'Who fixed that bandage?' Cleary asked turning to Shelby. 'Sit down man! Good God! I'll have you on my hands again if you don't treat yourself better.'

Kent sank wearily on to a horse-hair sofa. 'Donna Hale. Her real name's Russell, incidentally. Mason Hale's not her father. He just took her in–'

The lawmen stared wide-eyed at this piece of news but the medico brushed it aside as of little consequence.

'Donna Hale, eh? Well if Miss Montago lives, reckon she'll owe it to Donna Hale – Russell.'

'You don't give much for her chances, Doc?' Shelby said.

Cleary took another look at the girl lying on the couch. He bent down and fussed over her, felt her pulse and examined the raw, ugly wound again. He straightened up at last and wiped his hands on a clean towel.

'Kind of funny, your bringing her in now, Shelby, and she brought you in last time!'

'Funny ain't exactly the word,' Tom Borden said in a dry voice.

'No! Of course not. I mean – peculiar –

strange. Her chances, gentlemen? I wouldn't give a plugged nickel for her chances. But you cain't always tell. The bullet has lodged close to the left lung. I'll have to get it out. Either then, or as an immediate result of the operation, is when she's most likely to go, if she is going.

'I'm not really equipped for this sort of thing, gentlemen. This is a life-and-death matter. She needs a surgeon at Sage Junction–'

'She'd die before we got her half-way there,' Shelby said. 'Over a hundred miles–'

Cleary nodded his balding head. 'I'm afraid you're right, Mr Shelby – I'll have to do the best I can.'

'You'll need help, Doc,' Kent said. 'It's the least I can do. You tell me what you want. I'll do it!'

'Tom,' Cleary said turning to the lawman. 'You and Vern get out of here and go some place. Shelby! You wash yourself clean at that hand-basin. You've got to get every bit of dirt and travel dust off you. When we're through with Miss Montago, I'll look at you.'

In the room at back of Henry Guyler's store, four men sat, to all intents and purposes playing poker.

This evening, however, the cards and chips were window-dressing for the benefit of any idle callers.

The real business of the day was the discussion of a more serious gamble than one involving a mere play with cards.

Jack Summers was talking and the other three listened attentively.

'She came into town yesterday afternoon,' the blacksmith said, 'and saw the "wanted" notices pinned all over the place. Reckon she figgered me out as bein' sympathetic to Shelby, or at least against Mason Hale.'

Guyler nodded his head and leaned his vast bulk forward over the table. 'Go on, Jack,' he grunted.

'She said she figgered on settin' out an' findin' Shelby to warn him that he'd been outlawed. Warn him against the law and Horseshoe as well, seein' as how Ward Reeves had upped and died–'

'Hell!' Guyler interrupted. 'Terry's already lit out to warn Sugar Loaf an' join up with them if he can–'

'Why, we didn't know that, Henry! Guess there hasn't been much chance to get together on this thing until now.'

'You say you helped her, Jack?' Brad Straw said, directing a thin stream of tobacco juice into the large brass cuspidor.

'Reckon so,' Summers replied. 'Told her to bring both her horses around the back well after dark. Saw to it that she'd got a six-gun, rations, water and such stuff. She knew

Shelby was trail-drivin' to Sage Junction an' she knew Donna Hale was along too, having had a bust-up with Horseshoe. She kinda figgered it out, or had a hunch, that Shelby and Donna would make for the hills, if Horseshoe came bustin' in.'

'How'd she figger all that out?' Jim Gil wanted to know.

'She's a woman, ain't she?' Brad Straw said, and that was answer enough.

'What happened after that seems pretty clear. I did offer to go with her but she'd gotten her mind fixed on some plan or idea. Next thing we know is today. Shelby coming in with Isobel shot bad, maybe bad enough to die, Tom Borden reckons.'

Jack Summers's big fists clenched and the muscles showed up like ropes on his hairy arms. 'Reckon if they done for her – them murdering bustards – well Shelby ain't goin' to be fightin' that crowd alone, anyway!'

'What you propose, Jack?' Guyler said. 'What you figger's goin' to happen? Horseshoe's comin' back to town–?'

The blacksmith nodded. 'They'll be back, Henry, mark my words, an' this is our chance to rig the play in favour of law and order for once. *Our* law and order! Reckon Tom Borden and Shelby cain't do much on their own–'

'What about Vern?' Straw said. 'He's supposed to have found the sheriff all trussed up at the old Sand Flats stage station!'

'Don't trust him all the same,' Guyler said.
'Me neither.'

Jack Summers looked up and his dark eyes
were bright. 'With us four settin' in, we can
even things up and clean that scum up once
and for all. You, Brad, an' you, Henry –
reckon you're married men, not like me an'
Jim, but your wives are not safe right here in
this town come pay-nights and Horseshoe
starts letting off steam!'

Jack Summers lifted the shining carbine
from the floor and patted it with a huge
hand. There was as strange look in his eyes.

'I've got a notion to taste blood, tonight,
boys. You see' – his voice cracked a little– 'I
– Miss Montago–'

Guyler's thick brows lifted. 'You mean you
wanta get spliced, Jack?'

Summers wiped his mouth and swallowed,
watching the men, half fearful that they were
laughing at him. Their gazes were bright,
steady and unwinking, but there was no
laughter here at his expense. 'Reckon it
hasn't gotten as far as that!' He laughed jerk-
ily. 'Guess Miss Montago don't even know
how I feel, but–'

Guyler pushed the cards to one side. All
pretence as a game was now given up. He
produced a printed bill of goods and turned
it over so that the plain side was uppermost.

From his vest pocket he withdrew a stub

of pencil and commenced sketching on the paper.

'Here's Main,' he told the intently watching men. 'These two lines here. There's Cross Street and your shop, Jack.' He marked a cross on the paper. 'Here's my store.' He marked another cross. 'Brad, reckon your saddlery's about there. Don't know what we're goin' to do with you Jim, 'cos your livery jest don't come into the picture.'

Jim Gil thrust a dirty finger at the sheet. 'The back of the feed-barn butts on to the side of the Grand,' he said, his voice sharp with excitement, 'and the roof levels are about the same within a foot or two.'

'Well?' Guyler said.

'The Hotel has a false front, don't it, Henry, lookin' plumb down on to the street?'

The men nodded, smiling suddenly.

'I'll get on to that roof with a long gun when you an' Jack say the word. You're right boys. If anythin's goin' to happen tonight, this is our chance to establish a little law and order.'

If Vern Hanson had felt the faint touch of the town's mood the previous night, he sensed it more strongly than ever this evening.

There was an even greater air of expectancy underneath the hubbub of voices and laughter.

But the deputy had something more

tangible than the mood of a town with which to concern himself. It was the mood of a man – Judge Winter – and Hanson knew that in a very few moments he would have to answer Winter's summons and have a final show-down.

This had been the fly in the ointment which Hanson had anticipated.

He knew that as soon as the news of his finding Borden had spread the rounds, Judge Winter would demand an immediate explanation. It had not been a part of their plans for Borden to have been found yet, or even alive.

Now, Vern glanced at the unsigned note in his hand. It read:

I HAVE HEARD THAT
THE SHERIFF IS BACK.
PLEASE EXPLAIN IMMEDIATELY.

It was not signed, but Hanson had received notes from Judge Winter before. Not that they ever contained anything incriminating. Only the recipient would understand the underlying significance.

Hanson lit a match and held it to the paper, watching it slowly burn away and fall as ash to the floor. There was something faintly symbolic in the action, the more so as Vern drew his gun and thrust a sixth cartridge into the empty chamber. He spun the cylinder once and eased down the hammer, returning the gun to holster, feeling relieved that Shelby and Borden were, at the moment, in the Grand Hotel.

Vern crossed the street at an angle. Already lights were appearing in windows and spilling on to the side-walk from open doorways.

The deputy did not attempt to disguise his objective as he walked slowly towards the outside staircase that led to Judge Winter's office and rooms above McGraw's store, a little way down the street.

One or two men nodded to him on the way and Vern returned their greetings.

He was figuring things out as he went. It was going to be dangerous to kill Judge Winter, yet it was going to be more danger- ous to let him live. There would have to be a fight brought about some way or another and Hanson would have to let Winter get the gun from his desk first. He, Vern, would only shoot in self-defence. At least that would be the story, or something like that. He knew Winter kept a gun in his desk-drawer, he had seen it there on one occasion. There might even be papers or letters that would show Winter's tie-up with Horseshoe. That would be something! Vern Hanson would have the esteem and support of people like Guyler, Brad Straw, Jack Summers. They had more than once hinted that the judge's methods were crooked; even insinuated that he was tied in with Mason Hale!

Vern laughed quietly. It might pay him in more ways than one to kill this man. In any case, Winter's mouth would have to be shut once and for all!

The street was becoming noisier every moment and this suited the deputy's plans. If no one heard the shot he would not have to make an explanation of the killing!

He drifted up the wooden staircase and found the outer door at the top unlatched. The one to Winter's office, however, was locked and Vern knocked gently, easing the gun in its holster as he waited.

The judge's heavily jowled, scowling, red face thrust itself round the door and when he saw who his visitor was the scowl became more pronounced.

'Come in, Hanson,' he rasped. 'Sit down. I've got some crow to pick with you!'

Hanson remained standing, surveying the other coolly, thumbs hooked in gun-belt.

'Reckon you mean about Tom Borden?' he said grinning.

'You're dam' right, I do,' Winter snarled. 'What's your game, eh? You figuring you can upset our plans now?...'

Vern was listening intently. Not to Judge Winter's harangue, but to the street sounds coming thinly through the curtained windows.

He had never listened like this before and was surprised at discovering how little noise penetrated into this well-furnished room.

He brought his mind back to bear on what Winter was saying.

'…Good God, man, I don't believe you're even listening! I tell you, our plans have gone too far for Hale and me to brook any interference or double-crossing from a tin-star deputy–'

'Now is the time,' Vern thought, as a bunch of riders came whooping down the street, one at least of the high-spirited punchers letting off his six-gun in the air.

For a split second, Vern thought it might be Horseshoe, but in any case the opportunity was too good to miss!

He drew his gun and thumbed back the hammer, fast enough to catch the irate judge on one foot and for a fleeting moment Winter stared at the forty-five's gaping hole, stark fear sending his face ashen and paralysing his body. Then he lunged forward to the open drawer in his desk and Vern Hanson fired once, twice, his shots coinciding with the last roar of the six-gun on the street.

He grinned thinly. It had been well timed. No one outside could possibly have heard the crash of his Colt in this closed room with all that din going on outside.

He sheathed the gun and stepped across

the fat body where it had fallen behind the desk and began a systematic search for papers and – why not? – money as well!

Chapter XIV

'It's A Trap!'

Shelby drank his whisky, aware of men's bright, uneasy glances. They watched him from the corners of their eyes when they thought he was not looking. And yet, in those covert glances was more than a suspicion of admiration. Tom Borden saw this, for all his prosaic outlook.

Talk, too, was uneasy, in that men spoke with their tongues whilst their minds probed ahead at something they knew would come as surely as the sunrise. And what the position would be then and how many folk were shot and killed meanwhile was a matter of some considerable concern.

He was a cool one, that Kent Shelby, they told each other. Everyone had known for hours now that sooner or later Mason Hale would make an appearance with his hard-case crew of killers. And yet the Sugar Loaf owner stood with the sheriff, as unconcerned as all get-out, calmly drinking, the most noticeable thing about him, apart from his detached air and his obvious recovery from the beating up, being the forty-five gun whose black butt protruded conspicuously from the holster on his shell-belt.

This was the Grand Hotel and always things were a little quieter, a little more circumspect. Only occasionally Zwight Fuller had to throw out a man who had taken too much liquor aboard and it was a long time now since the sawn-off shot-gun, which everyone knew reposed under the counter, had been used.

Farther down the street, at the Last Frontier, there were no inhibitions and no holds barred and waves of revelry came surging up the night-enveloped street, rendered thin and discordant by distance and paradoxically in some way, laying restraint on the men in the Grand.

It was as though the bawdy laughter from the other end of town was a kind of sacrilege at such a time as this. Time! That was the important thing at the moment, men thought, as their glances lifted to the clock on the wall above the bar. It was nine-thirty and apart from the uproar earlier on caused by some of the Flying Wagon Wheel boys coming into town, apart from that, things at this end of Main had been fairly quiet. For a Saturday night!

Borden said, sipping his drink, 'Cleary's a clever son-of-a-gun. He sure patched you up all right. Maybe he'll be able to do something for Miss Montago.'

217

Shelby nodded and poured another small measure, carefully, with a rock-steady hand, into each glass.

'There's no lawful way to handle this thing, from now on, Tom,' he said quietly. 'Your badge, like I said once before, is no longer big enough to use for a shield. And what about those "wanted" notices?'

Borden snorted his disgust. 'They've all been pulled down and destroyed 'cept maybe the one that's supposed to be nailed up on your ranch-house. Vern says Judge Winter and Horseshoe forced him into this, but I've got as much backing from Cottonwood as Winter has. I'll have to see him and get the thing hammered out. I dunno. Looks like if your hunch is right, Kent, things'll be a mite different tomorrow.

'I know this much. Both of us, in a different way, are walking a tight-rope an' one wrong move'll see us in the dirt!

'This is the final show-down, Kent. It's been building up for a long time. A long time before you came. It just needed such a brash young fool as you to set a match to the powder!'

'You'd best stay out of this, Tom,' Shelby said. 'Unless you can deputize half the town to back you up, and I cain't see that happening. You want to get yourself killed for the sake of a tin star?'

Borden's head moved slowly from side to

side, but there was an obstinate set to his jaw.

'Guess no man's anxious to fling his life away or get himself crippled for the rest of his days. But unless I can help in stopping Horseshoe from going berserk my job'll be jest about finished, if nothing worse. Reckon if Hale busts this town open, Kent, they'll send Uncle Sam in to clean up the mess and yours truly'll be cleaned up in the process!'

'You mean a U.S. marshal?'

The sheriff nodded grimly. 'May even move in troops if they figger things is bad enough. You know what happens to towns and their sheriffs then?'

'I've seen it before, Tom. That's why I say you'd better stay out of this. One man, two men, even wearing badges cain't face up to a mob like Horseshoe when they've tasted blood. If Chip Bander and his crew are any indication of what Hale's like–'

A sudden noise in the hotel foyer caused all sound to cease abruptly in the bar. Booted feet echoed quickly across the floor until they reached the batwing doors.

A grey-haired man entered and surveyed the tensely silent crowd. Only the ticking of the clock broke the heavy silence until the newcomer spoke.

Sam Salmons of the Pothook spread let his glance fall on Shelby and the sheriff.

'Heard somethin' of the ruckus that's bin goin' on, Tom,' he drawled. 'Jest got into town. Thought you might like to know there's about six riders burnin' leather fer town from the valley.' He grinned. 'Couldn't see their brands. Wasn't thet close, but I'd figger they was Horseshoe.'

'Thanks, Sam,' Borden said quietly. 'Better get your boys off the street. There's liable to be some shootin'.'

Sam Salmons nodded and withdrew.

Tom Borden surveyed the men at the bar and glanced at Kent for a lead.

Shelby said, 'You men had better stay close to your drinks. I don't aim to bring the fight in here. Reckon you'd best stay, too, Tom. Maybe if you could find Vern it would be a help.'

They watched the tall, lean man as he drew his gun and checked the load before re-sheathing the Colt, and when Shelby's glance came up again there was a cold quality about the blue-grey eyes that made men wonder whether this fool had a chance after all.

And before Kent could turn, a man stepped away from the bar unleathering his own gun and handing it to the Sugar Loaf owner. 'Hey, Kent. One gun ain't much use against that lot. Take mine, it's a good one!'

A smile touched Shelby's lips briefly and was gone. 'Thanks,' he said and pushed his way through the batwing doors, walking leisurely towards the street.

He stood to one side of the hotel entrance for a few moments, accustoming his eyes to the darkness. Faintly he could hear the distant drumming of hooves and for a moment his mouth went dry. He touched the new plaster across the bridge of his nose, the one Doc Cleary had fixed after attending to Isobel. He had asked Cleary for black plaster this time and the medico had smiled.

'White shows up some, in the dark, Shelby,' he had said.

Now Kent was aware that the street was empty at this end. In the few minutes since Sam Salmons had ridden in the thronged side-walks had cleared. One or two saddle-horses still stood at hitch-racks. Apart from that and the low sullen roar from the Last Frontier and beyond, it was like a ghost town.

Shelby stood motionless in the shadows and tensed at the suddenness and closeness of the voice.

'We're sidin' you, Shelby. Keep on Main if you can!' The voice was Henry Guyler's and Kent glimpsed the dark shadow that spread itself against the door of Guyler's store and then was gone.

His gaze probed the street on either side, up and down, and once he thought he glimpsed the shine of a gun-barrel on the corner of Cross Street.

So Guyler was backing his play and by the look of things, Guyler was not alone! This was unexpected help and Kent felt a greater confidence stir within him.

The riders were near now, the hoof-beats, like drums, rising to a crescendo. Once or twice a man's voice lifted above the moving pocket of sound, but elsewhere the silence was heavy, until somewhere across the street a man's step sounded and then was still.

They came in suddenly, racing up an alley and hitting Main with the force of an explosion.

Shelby had moved into the deeper shadows and now his eyes fixed themselves on Mason Hale's huge figure in the lead. There was no doubt as to the identity of the man leading that wild bunch and for a second Frank Minden's bearded face showed in a shaft of light as he turned in the saddle. Kent thought he recognized Gunn, the man who had roped him. Then Hale's roar rose above the sound of milling riders.

'Loose a few shots, Pen, and show 'em we mean business. You, Cashman! Throw some lead on the other side!' The next few seconds were one blazing, crashing roar as carbine slugs tore into windows and doors on either side of the street. Suddenly the shooting stopped and with it all other sounds. Even the Last Frontier and the red light district waited with bated breath in a hushed silence.

'All right, folks!' Hale roared. 'It's Kent Shelby we want! Better come out, Shelby, before we bust the town wide open!'

Shelby deliberately cocked the hammer of his six-gun, knowing that the tell-tale, metallic click would carry through the stark silence.

Immediately he threw himself forward on to the board-walk in the dark shadows of a water-butt and instantly lead began crashing all around, tearing and splintering the wood-work behind him and breaking windows farther along the street.

Kent's right elbow was on the walk, his left hand outthrust to steady himself. He took careful aim and fired and his gun was the signal it seemed for others to open up.

Again the night air was torn with the bark of guns and the scream of ricocheting bullets. A carbine chattered from somewhere over Guyler's Store and one of Horseshoe's riders screamed and pitched from his horse.

Kent fired again and moved quickly back behind the water-butt as lead came at him. Then a carbine opened up from Cross Street and Kent was suddenly aware of a rifle cracking from overhead, somewhere, he figured, on the roof of the Grand!

Another Horseshoe rider swayed in his saddle, clutching his side, and panic seized them for a time, as horses reared and pranced, in the cross-fire of screaming lead.

'It's a trap!' A Horseshoe rider yelled and Mason Hale pointed to an alleyway, shouting for the men to follow.

As they swept by, dark, quick moving figures in the uncertain light, Shelby's gun came up and one man's racing horse moved across his gun-sights. Frank Minden!

For a thought-flash, the bearded face had been visible in a light cast from the board-walk, and Shelby had fired at the man he had more cause to hate than even Hale himself.

It was a snap-shot and a chance in a hundred and yet the bullet found Minden's body in that split second before he was able to gain the protection of the dark alley a few yards ahead.

Kent saw the man's figure jerk in the saddle and saw the horse swerve violently to one side. Before Kent could fire again the carbine from Cross Street spoke again and the bearded Horseshoe rider threw up and pitched from the saddle. Unable to extricate one foot from the stirrups, Minden was dragged through the dust by the frightened animal.

Kent stood up slowly and was aware that men were moving up behind him. He heard Tom Borden's voice calling and slowly turned.

'You all right, Kent? Good! Looks like you had some unexpected help! Where the hell's Vern–?'

His words were cut off sharply by the suddenly close-spaced shots, coming from the darkness of the street farther up. A man's voice carried down, but the words were indistinct and robbed of form and meaning by the rataplan of hooves which broke in sharply and quickly drummed away to nothing in the black distance.

'They've wheeled back on to Main,' Shelby said. 'That took some nerve–'

'Yeah! an' someone else's bin shot!' a man grunted.

'Henry, Brad, Summers!' Borden roared at the top of his voice. 'Get your horses!' He turned to one or two men standing close behind. 'Get your mounts men. I want twen'y riders an' I aim to get 'em if I have to shoot 'em first!'

'Kent! You stay here in the Grand an' wait till we git back. We're goin' after Hale and this time we're bringing him back, dead or alive!'

Henry Guyler emerged from the store, a sly grin on his sweaty face. From across Main, Jack Summers approached, a carbine in the crook of his arm. From the alleyway beside the Grand came Jim Gil and a few moments later, Brad Straw emerged from the saddlery.

Within fifteen or twenty minutes Tom Borden had gathered his posse, numbering some twenty-odd men. With a few last instructions hurled over his shoulder to Shelby, he wheeled his horse, raking it lightly with his spurs, and galloped away with the posse thundering at his heels.

It was Pen Winkler who first saw the buzzards wheeling over the hills to the north-west and Mason Hale's temper flared and colour stained his cheeks a deeper roan.

'If it's that fool, Bander,' he snarled, 'he asked for it, lighting out on his own. Come on men. We'll have to find out what's there!'

They rode as hard and as fast as they dared, as the twisting rocky trails would allow; Hale up in the front with Pen Winkler. Behind, came the other Horseshoe hands, including Fish Wilder, Bill Gunn, Frank Minden and Cashman.

They came on the faint, criss-crossed trails, and broke through the brush-choked rocks where Isobel Montago's horse had gone before, and where now Chip Bander's almost unrecognizable body lay, stiff and stark in the bloody dust.

Winkler looked up suddenly from the tracks he had been studying.

'They bin here, right enough, boss. Looks like Chip found 'em and lost out!'

'He lost out all right, the damned fool,'

Hale gritted, and the only trace of regret in him was because Shelby and the girl had outsmarted them.

'Where to now, boss?' Fish Wilder drawled.

Mason Hale's big body moved in the saddle as he swung his glance round to Cashman, the 'breed.

'Now's your chance to earn some money, Cashman,' he breathed, 'if you can make anything of these tracks!'

Cashman's black eyes travelled over the scene as he motioned Pen Winkler and Mason Hale back, so that whatever sign there was would not become trampled out completely.

Horseshoe watched, sitting their mounts in a rough arc, whilst Cashman slipped from leather and studied each piece of ground carefully before going on.

He found where Isobel's horses had entered the clearing and a little farther away where Chip Bander's big bay had come up. Cashman knew the bay's prints although they were faint and later on became lost in the scuffed-up dirt.

Taking the roughly defined trail on which Bander's mangled body lay, Cashman moved back, slowly and surely until he had disappeared from view amongst a jumbled mass of rocks and boulders.

They heard his sharp grunt of satisfaction even though they could not see him and

Hale stirred impatiently and would have spurred the horse forward if the brash Fish Wilder had not laid a restraining hand on Hale's arm.

For a moment it looked as though the Horseshoe owner's temper, barely held in restraint, would flare, to Wilder's cost, but Winkler said, 'He's comin' out, boss. He's shore found something!'

Cashman walked slowly and carefully towards them, his gaze on the ground, cutting a swathe from left to right as he walked and then suddenly moving ahead.

It was a tough chore, even to such an experienced tracker as the 'breed and minutes crawled by and built themselves into an hour, two hours, before Cashman's picture was sufficiently complete to offer as a solution to the problem.

He stood by Mason Hale's stirrup at last and spoke in his slow, clipped way.

'Shel-bee and Miz Donna come here. That's sure, boss. Chip come in too. Another rider, mebbe, over there–' Cashman's arm pointed to the thick clump of brush.

'Reckon a woman leading a hoss. Light tracks. Horse killed Chip, mebbe you can see. Single tracks pointin' away from those rocks where Shel-bee and girl made camp.'

'Go on, Cashman, dam' you!'

The 'breed's eyes flickered but he would not be hurried.

'Horse reared there, mebbe shot at. Most likely. Girl fell–'

'Donna?' Hale rasped.

Cashman shook his head. 'Know her pinto. Tracks okay leadin' from camp. Miz Donna gone!'

'What else, Cashman?'

'One horse carry double load. Make get-away there!' Again the 'breed pointed.

'Mebbe guesswork,' he admitted, 'but figger Shel-bee took girl wounded, mebbe dead. Tracks point for town, but that don't mean nothin'.'

'What other woman would be here except Donna?' Hale asked his crew in general. But blank faces and shrugs only answered him.

'You say Donna took out from here, Cashman? You're dead sure?'

The 'breeds black glance lifted to Hale's anger-stained face.

'Woman rode her pony, travellin' north-west. Jest figger it was Miz Donna, boss. Cain't say more.'

Pen Winkler said. 'Could be someone come to warn them we was on their trail. Chip comes up unexpected an' they fight. Shelby's horse kills Chip, but the woman, whoever it could be, was killed or wounded. Like Cashman says, Shelby takes her up on his sorrel and Donna rides off some place else. That right, Cashman?'

The 'breed nodded slowly. 'Is like I figger,

Pen,' he replied.

'Where the hell would Shelby have gone? Can't we trail him if he's carrying a double load?'

Cashman said. 'He's had good start and tracking not possible all way. Here is loose earth, dust, brush. Easier to cut sign. Further on you lose trail easy, even with double load.'

Hale thought a moment and glanced at the sun. Then at his men. He suddenly realized it had been a long time since anyone had eaten. These men would not fight so well on empty bellies. Besides, he must pull off three or four more men from the range and send them out after the Sugar Loaf trail-herd. He would strike them if nothing else. Then another thought occurred to Mason Hale. Cashman had said the tracks of a doubly laden horse pointed to town. He had said it didn't mean a thing. But what if it were taken on its face value? Suppose Shelby had risked his neck to get a wounded woman, or maybe a youngster, Terry Guyler for that matter, back to town? It was just the sort of crazy thing a fool like Shelby would do.

By God! That was about it! Terry Guyler had come up and been shot. Killed or wounded. Shelby had sent Donna on, maybe back to the trail-herd to tell the riders, and had taken the chance of going back to Warpath, in order to get help for the kid!

Hale recognized that part of it was sheer

guesswork, but it fitted in with Cashman's findings and Pen Winkler's observations. It also fitted in with Mason Hale's understanding of the type of man he had to deal with. Shelby had not scared before. Not even after Chip and the men had nigh on killed him. He had stubbornly refused to quit. Had even organized a trail-herd in complete defiance of anything Horseshoe had said or done!

Yes! Kent Shelby was the kind of dam'-fool character who would ride boldly into town for the sake of a sentimental whim!

Hale jerked his head suddenly.

'We'll get back to the ranch, boys. We all need food and a piece of rest. You, Fish, ride on to the north-west section. Who did Chip have working that stretch?'

Wilder thought for a moment.

'Reckon Jim Steen and Fred Venner. Yeah! Mebbe Shorty's with 'em, too.'

'All right, Fish,' Hale said. He had more control of himself now. Things were merely being postponed. He would have his fill tonight and so would the boys, if his hunch were right about Kent Shelby. And he was dam' sure it was right!

'Get Steen, Venner and Shorty, Fish, but first fill up with a meal. Then light out to the north of the hills and cut the cattle trail to Sage Junction.'

'Sure.' Fish Wilder's face was sweaty with anticipation.

'Break that trail-herd up if you have to kill every dam' steer to do it. Get those three riders Shelby has working for him!'

'What about Miss Donna if she's there?'

Hale's face was ugly. 'Bring her back. I'll deal with her,' he said in an unnaturally soft voice.

Chapter XV

Action By Night

By the time Horseshoe had returned to the ranch the sun was moving down the western end of the valley.

Fish Wilder had gone on ahead, had eaten a meal and saddled a fresh horse.

Now the rest of the crew, having eaten well, rested in the bunkhouse until Hale should be ready to lead them to town. Each man was to get a cash bonus if – or rather, when – they had settled with Shelby.

Mason Hale had thoughtfully sent a full bottle of whisky to the bunkhouse and already the contents were more than half gone.

The Horseshoe riders, now inflamed by the raw spirit, were anxious to ride down on Warpath and shatter the town from end to end. They figured there would be plenty of chance for this. Even if Shelby were there as Hale seemed to think, they could not see him walking out meekly into their arms!

Word came from the ranch-house to be ready to go and men hefted their saddles on to fresh mounts and checked their carbines and six-guns.

Yet it was well into evening when Hale called Pen Winkler and told him he was ready to move, and Pen, from the corner of his eye, watched Hale make a couple of tries for the saddle on the big gelding, before finally getting aboard.

They tore off through the night, wild, rough-and-tumble men that they were, beating the floor of the valley with the hoof-beats of their racing ponies.

Thus it was that Sam Salmons had glimpsed them from way ahead and thus it was, presently, that they smashed into town only to be met by stubborn and accurate opposition in what was virtually an ambush!

It was when Hale was leading his depleted riders down the alley that he thought of doubling back and so perhaps foxing any chance posse which might have gathered in sudden defiance of Horseshoe.

And Hale might well have pulled it off, with the posse travelling north in the darkness, had he not glimpsed the shadowy, star-decked deputy, Vern Hanson, on the edge of the board-walk along Main.

Even on hitting town, Hale had subconsciously noted that the white posters were no longer apparent. Coupled with the surprise attack on Horseshoe it savoured of a double-cross.

Hale did not know that Tom Borden was

back but he did know that someone here in town had gotten together, not merely to obstruct Horseshoe but, judging by the carbine fire, to cut them to pieces.

Seeing Hanson in the glimmer of light on the board-walk was sufficient to pin-point the traitor in the camp, as far as Hale was concerned, and regardless of the cost he savagely neck-reined the gelding in order to find out from Vern what had happened. He had no doubt that Vern had played a double game now and with gun already drawn, he turned his wrathful gaze on the deputy's figure.

Vern saw the drawn gun, had indeed heard most of the shooting down the street and had hoped to re-emerge in the town during the general confusion.

The meeting, however, was so unexpected as to shock Hanson into momentary rigidity. But only for a moment. Light winked on the drawn gun in Hale's fist and the deputy went for his gun.

It was scarcely clear of leather before Hale's shots had echoed down the street and Vern spun round like a whipped top and fell head forward into the dust of the street, his booted feet caught in the bottom step of the side-walk.

With a few shouted words to his men, Hale raked the gelding's flanks and thus Shelby, farther down the street was able to indicate to Borden that Hale was going east and not north.

Frank Minden was dead and left behind in Warpath. Pen Winkler was wounded but was clinging gamely to his horse. Bill Gunn, too had gone down in the town's bloody dust and only Cashman rode beside them, cool and unperturbed, easy in the saddle as only a born horseman can be.

Cashman now raised his voice above the din of flying hooves. 'Fan out, boss. Best chance'; and without waiting for permission the 'breed turned his pony and let the night-range swallow him from view.

The man who had given Shelby his six-gun now clapped him on the shoulder.

'Nice work, Kent,' he grinned. 'Reckon you've earned a drink tonight. What do you say boys?'

The crowd voiced its approval in no uncertain manner and suddenly Shelby thought, 'My God, it's all over!'

'There's a couple of Horseshoe riders by the alley, men,' he said. 'The bearded one's Frank Minden, I think, and maybe a pilgrim called Gunn is farther down. Figure we'd best clean the street up first.' He handed the six-gun back to the man who announced his name as Jakes.

'The boys'll see to thet chore, Shelby. You've earned some rest and quiet. Git back to the Grand and order what you fancy!'

Kent grinned and passed a rough hand over his sweaty face. He realized for the first time that his legs were trembling and his side ached like hell.

'Reckon I could use one,' he said and walked slowly and carefully along the walk as though unsure that his legs would successfully take the weight of his body.

It was a long session even for a Saturday night in Warpath, but Kent managed to avoid too much liquor. There was something he wanted to do before settling down in the hotel to wait for the sheriff's return.

He heard the church clock strike midnight as he walked the short distance to Doc Cleary's cottage and was mildly surprised that the hour was so late. There were now, once again, quite a few punchers, miners and the like, drifting along the walks and lights showed up in saloons and dance-hall and stores as well, where, no doubt, the interrupted poker games were once more in full swing.

As there was a light still going in the medico's cottage, Shelby did not hesitate to knock and the doctor himself came to the door. When he saw his visitor, he motioned him inside and looked sharply at the Sugar Loaf owner. Shelby's face was drawn and lines of fatigue showed white in the lamplight.

'Mrs Cleary and I managed to get her upstairs into a spare room, Shelby,' Cleary said. 'She's still alive. That's about all I can say.'

Kent nodded. 'Reckon you heard shooting, Doc. Horseshoe's more or less busted up. We got Frank Minden and Bill Gunn in town. Hale and a couple of others lit out. Borden's after them with a posse.'

Cleary nodded. 'One of the town men came by earlier and told me more or less what happened. You go home now, Shelby, or better still stay over in town. I'll see you tomorrow when you've had some rest.'

Zwight Fuller waddled towards Shelby as soon as the latter entered the hotel.

'There's a lounge chair right here in the lobby, Mr Shelby, if you're figgerin' on staying up, or you kin have a room and a bed upstairs. No charge!'

Kent smiled and sank into the padded, cane lounge-chair. 'Thanks. I'll take this and just loosen my belt. Want to be on hand when Tom Borden gets back.'

'Sure,' Zwight grunted. 'Can I get you something? Cup of cawfee maybe or chocolate?'

'Cup of chocolate sounds good, Zwight. Guess I'll settle for that and a cat-nap!'

Fuller nodded and padded away and Shelby relaxed his throbbing body in the chair, unbuckling his gun-belt and spurs and crossing booted feet on the stool, thoughtfully provided for tired customers.

Presently fat Zwight returned with Shelby's chocolate and spoke to the pimply night clerk still on duty.

'You go off now, Len. I'll take over for the rest of the night.'

'Okay, Mr Fuller,' the clerk replied and staggered tiredly up the staircase towards the rooms above.

Zwight sank his massive bulk into an overstuffed chair behind the reception desk and was almost instantly asleep.

Through the screen door Shelby could see the street darken quickly as though all those inhabitants still out of bed had simultaneously realized their sudden fatigue.

He rolled a quirly and slitted his gaze against the ascending spiral of smoke, pushing his thoughts out to the cattle trail and wondering whether Cal and Charlie and Terry had been able to cope. Wondering also whether Donna had joined up with them and suddenly feeling anxious about them all.

He finished his cigarette and chocolate and dozed; but it was more than that, really, because it was the sound of hooves that awoke him and the toneless pitch of men's voices when they are physically exhausted.

Kent stretched his stiffened muscles and eased himself from the creaking chair. It was almost light outside but the sun had not yet climbed above the eastern rim.

He shivered a little at the cool fresh air as he stepped out on to the board-walk. Down the street came the tired riders. Horses dusty and lathered, hastening now a little as they sensed a warm, hay-filled stable.

Borden was at the front and his hand lifted as he sighted Shelby.

'Never bin so dam' tired in all my life, Shelby,' he said, dismounting and throwing his reins to Jim Gil.

'What of Mason Hale?' Shelby's face was taunt and hard like his voice.

Tom Borden's glance came up, sharply, and with a sudden, rare insight he read the physical and mental strain that had pulled at Shelby for so long.

'He's at the bottom of Rock Creek. A fitting place–'

'More fitting than you think, Tom, when you consider he pushed Gus Garner there. Now he's found the same grave unless he gets fished out by someone.'

'Hell, Shelby! You got proof–? Not that it matters now.'

Kent smiled. 'I hadn't until last night, but we can go into that later. Looks like Zwight had better get some breakfast ready for you right now.'

Borden said, 'We won't disturb him. The Chink restaurant's already open. We'll get grub there.'

He turned to follow the men and Guyler and Straw rode by with Jack Summers. Their glances came at Shelby in the growing morning light and the men grinned as Kent's hand lifted in salute.

'Thanks, men,' he said and the others nodded, following the weary posse to the Chinese restaurant.

Later the sheriff returned and found Shelby in the dining-room of the Grand, partaking of a late breakfast.

'Have some coffee, Tom,' Kent said indicating the pot and a spare cup on the table.

The sheriff sat down and poured the black liquid, which he drank in noisy gulps. Afterwards he wiped his moustache with the back of a dusty hand.

'Hale took a wrong turning right enough. Galloped along a ledge that ended plumb sudden 'bout hundred feet above Rock Creek. Last we saw even the gelding was going down and Hale's hat was the only thing afloat.'

'What about the others?'

'Pen Winkler was bad wounded. We overtook him not long out of town. Two of the men stayed with him but he was dead when we came back. Reckon the other *hombre* was Cashman the 'breed. He jest natcherally vanished. Reckon we won't see hide or hair of him again! What now, Kent?'

241

Shelby sat back and rolled a smoke, passed the makings to Borden.

'The boys found Minden and Bill Gunn. Frank was a nasty sight so I'm told. They also took care of Vern's body. He had two bullets in him, reckon from Hale's gun. Hale figured Vern was two-timing, which he was, inasmuch as he "found" you. That one smells, Tom. It was a put-up job if ever there was one. Vern was playing both ends against the middle. Judge Winter, Mason Hale and the law. It looks like he killed Winter. Maybe I forgot to tell you that, Tom!'

Borden smiled grimly. 'We heard soon as we hit town.'

Kent nodded. 'He's down at Cleburne's complete with money and papers rifled from Winter's office. Those papers kind of tie up with my theories.'

'Let's have it, Kent!'

'Hale was in partnership with Winter. He didn't like it much because Hale wanted to be king-pin around here. However, it looks like the judge had a pull on Mason. Hale killed his old partner and robbed him of a sizeable poke. Russell was the man's name. He had a daughter called Donna–'

'Donna?'

Kent nodded. 'Donna Hale is really Donna Russell. Why Hale took her in I don't know, but he did. Gus Garner let out that there was copper on Sugar Loaf and since that day

Hale's been determined to get it, whatever the cost. It looks like he fixed with Chip to follow Garner to Three Forks and kill him for the deeds. They found Gus drunk, undoubtedly, but he'd already sold the ranch to me!'

'What then?'

'Guess they figured, quite reasonably, that Gus had already sold to Johnnie Montago. The deeds were not on Garner when Chip and the boys found him; they didn't know about me then, so they concluded Gus had fixed it with Johnnie. So Hale or Bander hire three cheap road-agents to knock off the miners' pay and get the deeds off Johnnie at the same time, knowing he's alone in the Wells-Fargo office. They picked a good time all right, killed Johnnie but again found no sign of the deeds. Then I come in. You know what happened after that. They've been after my hide and the ranch ever since. Now I'm getting back to the trail, Tom, and see if I've got a crew and a herd left.'

'Where's Donna, now, Kent?'

'She should have joined up with Cal and Charlie. Terry Guyler's with them too.'

'Anythin' else?'

'One other thing, Isobel Montago saved my life and risked her own to warn me and Donna. Doc's a good man, but if she should want anything, anything at all, Tom, even if it means riding to Silverbell or Cottonwood–'

'You don't have ter say any more, Kent,' Borden assured him, 'and while we're on the subject – look after Donna!'

The prospect of a big bonus spurred Fish Wilder to great efforts, and with a good meal under his belt and a couple of drinks, he set out on a fresh pony for the north-west section.

Night riding for any of the Horseshoe crew was no chore at all. They knew their own particular range and a surprising area of other ranges. A few cattle could always be run off on the side and the brands changed, without interfering too much with their routine work.

Therefore, Wilder pointed his mount across the range over trails that existed in his mind only. They were not beaten paths like roads or even tracks, but he knew the shortest distance between two points and what is more he knew what lay between.

Thus, he was able to avoid the steeper-sided, earth bottomed barrancas, which at night might well prove disastrous to a rider ignorant of their existence.

Wilder figured that one of the men at least would be at the line-cabin and it was towards this distant spot that Fish headed out. Due west were the hills and he knew that if they travelled due north-west, they could cut the Sage Junction cattle trail at any point they chose.

It was close to midnight before the Horse-shoe rider glimpsed the faint light ahead, showing that someone was still up and about in the northern line-cabin. Cattle were visible, bedded down in shallow dips, one or two bawling protests as Wilder's pony clattered over stretches of shale or stones.

Fish saw the rider then, even as the man hailed him, and Fish shouted 'Horseshoe!' and trotted up to Jim Steen.

'Howdy, Jim,' he drawled. 'Leave this bunch of steers. We got work to do!'

Steen neck-reined his horse and both men put their mounts towards the line-cabin.

'What's doin', Fish?' Jim Steen said presently and Wilder gave him a brief outline of the events which had led up to Mason's decision to ride to town and at the same time strike at Sugar Loaf's trail-herd.

'You got Fred here, Jim?' Wilder asked presently.

'Yep, an' Shorty too. They're both inside playin' cairds,' Steen grinned. 'They won't like leavin' that nice warm, comfortable game.'

'They will when they hear about the bonus, Jim,' Wilder grunted, sliding from leather and ground-hitching the pony.

A man came to the now open door of the lamp-lit cabin, light gleaming on the gun in his hand.

'It's me, Fred,' Jim Steen called, 'and Fish. He's got work for us!'

They entered the cabin, heavy with the smell of men, tobacco and whisky. The reek of kerosene was almost pleasant by comparison.

Wilder reached for a half-empty bottle, moistening his throat, as he said, with a little of the liquor.

Shorty, the round, barrel-shaped member of the party, looked up sharply from under bushy brows. 'What we gotta do, Fish, and how much do we get?'

Wilder grinned and his teeth showed very white against the saddle-leather of his face and the thick black moustache along the upper lip.

'We'll ride out soon and cut the cattle-trail by dawn or soon after. We look out for Sugar Loaf's trail-herd – should be easy enough to find – and jest natcherally send it to hell-an'-breakfast.'

'How many riders we up against?' Fred Venner demanded suspiciously.

Fish took another drink and smiled.

'Three oldsters, and a boy, Terry Guyler. We figger Donna's there as well, but we don't kill her. We bring her back!'

'Cain't we–'

Wilder brought his fist down on to the table with a crash that threatened to upset the lamp as well as the liquor.

'You can cut that out, Shorty, less'n you want Hale to slit your throat!'

'You brought plenty of shells?' Jim Steen asked practically.

Fish nodded. 'Enough to kill that bunch o' bustards a dozen times over. Somebody rustle up some grub an' let's eat, an' leave enough to pack in your saddle-bags!'

Later, carbines and six-guns were checked and loaded and Fish Wilder handed out another fifty rounds apiece. The horses were watered and cinch-straps tightened and the four men pulled on leather jackets against the cold night air.

They moved out across the range, dark, shadowy figures with dark purpose in their hearts and thoughts of gold in their minds.

Chapter XVI

Trouble On The Trail

Both the sorrel and its rider were rested, though Shelby's face still bore obvious signs of strain.

Yet he had slept, he knew, quite deeply, in the foyer of the hotel and a late breakfast had imbued him with strength enough for the long ride ahead.

Guyler came along the side-walk as Kent untied the sorrel's reins from the rack.

'I haven't thanked you properly yet, Henry,' Shelby said, but Guyler waved it aside with a sweep of his arm.

'We've been needing a chance to clean things up, Kent,' he said. 'It was jest that you gave us that chance. Terry's with you. He all right?'

'I hope to God they're all of them all right, Henry, and that they're well on the way to Sage Junction. I'm figuring on cutting across Horseshoe land. It's shorter and should be quiet now.'

Guyler nodded. 'You take the north-west trail, Kent, it'll bring you along the other side of the twin buttes. Bear more west after that and you'll have the copper-hills to the back of you. That brings you north, on the other side of the hills and you can cut the trail where you want.'

Kent nodded and climbed into leather.

'I'm not particularly expecting trouble now, but I'll be anxious to get the herd to Sage and the crew back to Sugar Loaf.'

Guyler raised his arm. 'Be seein' you, Kent.'

Shelby rode, as before, in the fashion of the Rangers and the U.S. Troopers. It was surprising the distance a man could cover across the range in this fashion. Most of the cowpunchers – that wild, salty breed – flogged their game little ponies until they were lathered and spent. Well enough for short distances but methods that were useless for a long ride!

He watched the landscape, his gaze on the horizon and distant washes for any sign of dust-clouds. But dust had stirred over the valley last night, with a vengeance. He did not look for a repetition of such as that.

He gauged the time by the climbing sun as being mid-way between nine and ten, when he glimpsed the deserted Horseshoe ranch buildings and began reining the sorrel in a more westerly direction. This way he would pass south of Horseshoe and north of the twin buttes and Sugar Loaf. Like Guyler had said, the copper-hills now lay on his left flank, in a west-south-westerly direction.

It was then that Kent noticed the faint tracks head. Track of a single horse that had been ridden easily, not more than twelve hours before, possibly less.

He dismounted and studied one or two of the more clearly defined prints. Already some were half filled and partially obscured by the fresh-blow dust. There was nothing remarkable at all about the fact that a rider had passed this way earlier on, unless it was that the sign pointed in the exact direction in which Shelby himself was travelling!

Still in the forenoon, Kent began searching for water. He gazed across the range with the field glasses and presently saw the log building which he rightly took to be one of Horseshoe's line-cabins. The northern line-cabin, he supposed. There would be water there, he thought, and food too if he wanted it. Such was the law of the range, so long as a man did not abuse it.

But perhaps the situation was a little difficult here. Horseshoe and Sugar Loaf were, or had been, at war and Kent had no way of knowing whether the cabin were inhabited or not, right now. No way of knowing, except that the tracks ahead continued to point in that direction.

Kent checked his six-gun and slid it back into leather. He touched the sorrel lightly with his spurs, riding forward with an unflurried sense of purpose.

There was no smoke coming from the chimney and his glance passed over the nearby grazing cattle, making sure there was no rider amongst them.

He immediately saw, however, on reaching the cabin that men had been there recently. Only the night before. Dirty glasses and an empty whisky bottle, apart from hastily scrubbed tin plates and opened cans, were ample evidence that a quick meal had been partaken of quite recently.

It vaguely puzzled and irritated Shelby, more especially as he considered the tracks of the single horse which had led straight to the cabin. But it was not until he had watered the sorrel at the nearby creek that he found where the other mounts had been tied, at the side of the hut. Here was evidence again that two horses, then two more, had stood for a time.

He squatted down on a rough bench outside the cabin and munched some jerky and soda crackers taken from his saddle-bags. He would take water for his horse from Horseshoe, but nothing else. Then he remembered, with a grim smile, that Mason Hale was dead, so what did it matter now anyway?

Yet the problem of the other riders gently nagged at him. These men were almost certainly Horseshoe riders, and even if Hale,

Minden, Winkler and Bander were all dead, might there not be a possibility–?

Kent rolled a quirly and washed down his meal with a few sips of water from the brim-full canteen. Smoking the cigarette he began searching the ground, walking round the cabin and scrutinizing the ground as carefully as any Ranger.

Soon he found where the four horses had headed out, the tracks though not clear, still faintly visible, and suddenly in spite of the burning, morning sun, a cold shiver ran through him as his mind leaped ahead at the sudden possibilities!

The sorrel, through careful handling, was as fresh as paint and in a few moments Shelby was astride its back and riding steadily to the north-west.

To the south-west, the copper-hills were slashes of green, blue and purple against the yellow-brown grass and smoke-grey sage. To the north stretched wild, ragged country, reminiscent of the Texas Panhandle. North-west was Kent Shelby's direction and somewhere ahead there, he would hit the cattle-trail to Sage Junction and find – what?

He must be at least eight hours behind the four riders ahead and a great deal could happen in that time, Kent figured, as he began to gauge how fast he dared travel without laming or lathering the sorrel.

Fish Wilder rode with a brash confidence and a newly born air of superiority which the other men found hard to stomach.

He had told Jim Steen to ride on fast and scout the way ahead and the older man's temper had roughened at the sudden change in Wilder's tone.

'Since when we taken orders from you, Fish?' Steen grumbled.

'Since last night, Steen.' Wilder's lean face darkened with sudden anger. Now was no time for any kind of insubordination.

'Hale himself told me what to do and I'm carrying out his orders in tellin' you, see?'

But Steen had gone on after his mild protest and Wilder resumed his former confident mood.

The sun was climbing the eastern sky when Fish called a halt for a dry camp. He was not in any hurry, knowing that the Sugar Loaf beef would still be a long way from the railroad town of Sage Junction. He could take that herd and crew just when and how he wanted. He was sure of that!

They were still drinking coffee which Shorty had boiled on the fire when they spotted a rider coming in from the northwest, about three miles away. Wilder, for all his confidence, did not relax or withdraw his hand from the six-gun until the newcomer had been identified as Jim Steen.

'Not far away, Fish,' Steen said dismounting and reaching for a cup of coffee.

'How far?' Wilder wanted to know.

'Reckon about fifteen-twen'y miles from here, Fish, though I went close up for a look-see. Anyways they ain't too far up the trail.'

Wilder nodded. 'Well there's no great hurry. Still maybe we'd best get on. Sooner it's done with, sooner we all collect!'

But the herd would not be easy to take because sharp eyes had spotted the distant figure of the watching rider, once when he had momentarily skylined himself.

It had been the keen eyes of the boy, Terry Guyler, who had first seen and he had raced his pony over to where Cal Eddy rode at point.

'May mean nothin', kid,' Eddy said thoughtfully, 'but it might mean one helluva lot! Sure wasn't Kent, anyway. Take my place for a bit, kid. I'm goin' to have a word with the others.'

But Donna, who had descended from the hills with unerring instinct and had joined up with the outfit the previous evening, had seen young Guyler turn in his saddle and stare, before riding over to Cal Eddy.

The girl had followed the direction of his gaze and had glimpsed the distant, watching horseman.

Some instinct had prompted Donna to reach for her glasses in her saddle-bag and before the rider had finally turned and disappeared from view, the green eyes behind the powerful lenses had identified the figure of Jim Steen.

An intuitive feeling of trouble came over her suddenly and with a glance at the now steadily swinging herd, she turned from her flank position and raced the horse towards where Harry Busch had now joined Colfax and Eddy.

She pulled up breathlessly beside the Sugar Loaf men.

'Terry say anything about that rider watching us, Cal?' She had to raise her voice to a near shout so that it would carry above the dull roar of the moving herd.

'Why, yes, Miss Donna,' Eddy drawled. 'Terry was kinda suspicious I reckon–'

'So am I, Cal,' Donna shot back. 'I put these glasses on him. That rider was Jim Steen of Horseshoe. Reckon it might mean that Hale has pulled men off the range to hunt us down?'

'By God,' Colfax shouted. 'That's as likely as not!'

Eddy put his gaze to the country ahead, leastways, what he could see of it through the hazy curtain of dust.

'Charlie,' he said at last. 'We gotta get this herd bedded down in a safe spot, and we've gotta move fast. We don't know whether we got an hour or a day!'

'Probably a little more than the one an' a dam' sight less than the other,' Colfax grunted pessimistically. 'What you want we should do?'

'We're goin' to divide the herd while it's movin', Charlie, if it's humanly possible. If it ain't, we'll still divide it. Better to sacrifice a hundred beeves than lose the whole three hun'ed! Listen! You, Harry an' Terry cut out the first hundred an' keep them on the trail. Donna an' me'll swing the others round an' try to bed them down in the nearest wash or likely spot. Then, with any luck, if Horse-shoe riders come down on us, the main herd'll be some miles behind us. 'Less they come in when we're doin' it, they won't know!'

'They'll find out soon enough when they come close in and see such a small herd, Cal,' Busch pointed out.

'Reckon they will, Harry, but by that time we'll be fightin' and no-one'll have time to start lookin' for the rest of the beeves!'

Busch nodded. 'We'll try it, Cal. We cain't lose much anyway.'

Colfax said, 'I'll tell Terry and we'll start cuttin' out the first hundred. You be right behind, Cal, ready to start turnin' the others off'n the trail. Miss Donna better stay with the drag till we git them beeves sorted out.'

Cal Eddy nodded, watching while Colfax and Busch put spurs to the ponies, racing ahead to start the work with Terry.

They sweated and swore and worked like niggers, coaxing, hitting, wheedling the dumb beasts to do as they wanted them. Each rider had a bandanna up to his eyes, but each face, including the girl's, was streaked with sweat and masked with trail-dust.

Colfax, with the help of Busch and Terry, cut the first hundred and kept them moving more or less easily along the broad trail. But Charlie had to let Terry go eventually and help with the large number of recalcitrant bests who could see no good purpose served in turning off the trail and leaving their companions to go on ahead!

'Surely,' Eddy thought, in his brief moments of sanity, 'the kid and the girl have won their spurs today if this dam', con-blasted herd ever gits to doin' the right thing!' Yet it was a lesson to see two cow-punchers, a miner, a girl, and a boy, bring order from chaos in so short a time.

Luck favoured them inasmuch as one mossy-horn, who had gotten a place for himself somehow or another in the herd, decided that the wide, deep ravine a half-mile away was just as good, if not better, than the hot, dusty trail with no bunch-grass to chew on occasionally.

The mossy-horn was placed in just about the right position and once Cal had turned him off the trail with a little gentle coaxing and swearing, the other steers, or most of them, began to follow, though with much reluctance.

But it was done at last and Eddy discovered that the cattle left behind were invisible from the trail, unless they decided to wander back up the shallow ravine. But there was good grass there and a more than even chance they would stay, at least for a while. The chance of a good graze after thirty-odd miles of trailing would hold them there for a time.

With the smaller herd ambling along, the crew could relax for a little while, just so long as they kept their eyes peeled for riders.

They sipped the luke-warm water in canteens whose metal fittings were hot to the touch and wiped sweat and dust from faces and necks.

Young Terry Guyler volunteered to ride well behind the dust of the small drag herd to keep an eye on their backtrail and Cal and Donna combed the two jobs of point and flank riders, one on either side. Colfax went on ahead to scout the way while Busch stayed with the moving herd and at about the time that Shelby found the remnants of Fish Wilder's dawn camp a rifle cracked from an outcrop of rocks on the Sage Junction cattle-trail and Charlie Colfax pitched from the saddle, a mile or so from the oncoming herd in whose path he now lay curiously sprawled!

By holding a tight rein on his mounting impatience, Shelby had brought the sorrel well and quickly in the wake of the four Horseshoe riders ahead.

He knew he must have considerably reduced the distance and time separating them.

The ashes of the fire were scarcely cold and imprints of men and horses were clear enough where the soil was powdery, away from the short brown grass.

He took time off to dismount and give the game horse a little water, which he poured into his hat from the half-filled canteen.

Then Kent rubbed the sorrel with a sweat rag, obliterating the tell-tale streaks of lather on legs, chest and withers.

His own body oozed sweat, in this almost shadeless terrain, and the woollen shirt was stained with great wet patches.

The sun would be hotter still, he knew, as it passed the noon mark but there was no time now to think of such discomforts and he pushed the sorrel into a fast lope.

He saw the dust stirring on the trail ahead; knew it to be denser than it should be from a slow-moving trail herd; knew then that trouble had struck the Sugar Loaf trail-crew!

He called forth the best from his horse then and the powerful animal responded, seeming to sense the urgent need for speed.

Soon he heard the crashing of carbines and now, with the dust rising, he was able to gaze down on the trail and anger rode him for a long moment urging him to ride down hell-for-leather into the scene of the attack.

The fact that there was no herd any longer, he dismissed with scarcely a thought. He had known that the herd had been stampeded and now he understood why.

He could see the glint of rifle barrels from the outcrop of rocks and made out the small darkly sprawled figure of a man. Somehow he sensed it was either Cal or Charlie or Terry. It was not Donna, of that he was sure.

Now Shelby's gaze swung out across the land, seeking dips and washes through which and along which he might approach unobserved.

This would be the best way to take them, he knew. If he could be close enough to line his sights on the attackers he could quite well tip the scales in Sugar Loaf's favour with one or two well-placed shots.

Quickly wheeling the sorrel, Shelby moved to the right, striking out at an angle and gaining the protection of a long dip of country, part screened with sage-brush and low bushes. He judged time and distance with a cool calculation, yet it was only a part of him that could weigh up things so clearly. For the rest, a spark had been kindled and now burst forth into a consuming flame of anger, bringing with it the desire to destroy these murderers ahead.

And as Shelby approached the farther end of the draw, he trailed the sorrel's reins and drew the carbine from its boot.

He crawled forward and raised his head above the lip of brush-screened ground and gazed down at the rocks now only seventy or a hundred yards ahead.

Crouched down he saw them, pointing their rifles to where the Sugar Loaf crew lay behind whatever cover they had been able to find. He saw something else as well as the four Horseshoe killers. It was the body of Charlie Colfax, identifiable now at such close range, and with a sudden cold purpose, dia-metrically opposed to his former hot anger, Shelby drew back the hammer of his carbine and slowly lined his sights on the nearest of the four men.

He fired and almost instantly the man jerked back from the rocks, his cry stillborn as he clutched at his bubbling throat. Slowly it seemed he keeled over and toppled from the ledge to fall in a grotesque shape on the oven-hot rocks lower down. But Shelby was not watching the tumbling man. He knew that his eye was straight and his finger steady on the trigger, and before the man had fallen Shelby's sights had swung on to the second one as he half rose and brought his rifle up.

Again the carbine barked and death's messenger came fast in the shape of screaming lead. A ragged cheer ascended from the trail and dimly Kent was aware of Cal's voice sounding off somewhere to the left.

But now the other two Horseshoe men had dipped down behind the rocks, badly frightened and not anxious to show their faces enough to shoot.

Kent rose, the Spencer cocked and ready in his hands, and like a relentless Nemesis, devoid of earthly fears and impervious to physical hurt, he walked down the slope, his face a sweat-stained mask, His eyes cold as stones.

Nearer, nearer he came and still neither man had the nerve to stand up and meet the coming of this deadly killer.

It was Fish Wilder at last who, in desperation, raised his head and shoulders above the rocks and in that split second Shelby dropped to one knee, firing Ranger-fashion, blazing away with the Spencer in a sudden, savage, berserk fit of fury.

Wilder died with five of the remaining eight carbine slugs in his body and Shorty threw down his guns and stood up, screaming for mercy.

Shelby was still coming on, now only ten yards away, and Shorty saw death staring him in the face for the first and last time.

Deliberately, Shelby drew his six-gun and emptied it into the fat, pot-bellied body.

'That's for Charlie Colfax you dirty, murdering swine!' His voice cracked suddenly and for a long moment he stood and stared with a fixed expression, until the red mists of passion slowly lifted from his eyes.

He had killed four men in as many minutes but their deaths would never restore Charlie Colfax to life!

Suddenly Kent sat down, exhausted and spent, and slowly he put his head in his hands and gazed at the ground with bowed head.

A week had gone by and much had happened.

Harry Busch had brought over a mining expert from the copper-mines and had spent a considerable amount of time each day going over Sugar Loaf land.

The upshot had been that, as far as they could tell, having dug down at several different places and examined samples of strata, there was no more likelihood of copper being here than anywhere else.

Gus Garner had created the idea, the better to make his hated neighbour, Mason Hale, jealous and angry.

Shelby had shrugged. It didn't matter

much. He had wanted the thing settled now and it was done with .The irony of it all lay in the fact that the innocent as well as the guilty had paid with their lives for land that was valuable only as good graze!

Donna, at the request of Henry Guyler and his wife, had gone to stay with them at the store for a while.

A cattle syndicate was negotiating with Donna for the purchase of Horseshoe as Tom Borden and most everyone else in town had ruled that Donna was the rightful heir.

Cal Eddy went about the ranch-work quietly, with the willing and earnest help of young Terry, and Kent paced moodily up and down thinking about the dead Charlie Colfax lying buried out on Sugar Loaf land and realizing that sooner or later he would have to face up to the future. Make a start, for instance, by going into town.

Yet another week slipped by before he could shake the demons of recrimination from his shoulders. Then he sent Terry into town for a glazier and carpenter and soon the battered ranch-house began to look spick and span, and Shelby dragged his mind from the limbo of the past, knowing at last that life had to go on, for all that a man had lost his friend in so terrible a fashion.

When Shelby finally got around to making the trip to Warpath, he found he was considered something of a hero.

Many of the townsfolk had bitterly resented Mason Hale's hold over the valley and the rough actions of Chip Bander's crew, but few had had the necessary strength or initiative to resist. Traders like Guyler, and Brad Straw, and the blacksmith and liveryman had been most prominent in their passive resistance.

But it had taken a man like Kent Shelby to inspire them and for that, and for what Kent and his small crew had done, most of them were grateful.

Some, too, had felt pressure from Judge Winter and these folk passed a silent vote of thanks to Vern Hanson, even though they now knew that Hanson had two-timed the law.

Kent extricated himself from the throng of well-wishers on the street and lifted a hand in salute to the nearby Tom Borden.

Then he made his way to Doc Cleary's cottage and without a word the medico took him upstairs and into a room flooded with summer sunshine and bedecked with gay flowers.

Shelby paused on the threshold. There was a big-boned, clean-shaven man already sitting in a chair by the bed. But Cleary pushed Kent into the room and closed the door behind him.

Isobel Montago's pale face turned and the blue eyes brightened and misted with tears.

'Don't take any notice of me, Kent,' she said. 'I cry awful easy these days. Everyone's been so good!'

Isobel must have realized Shelby's awkwardness when his glance travelled to the man by the bed. He looked up and said ''Lo, Kent,' and Shelby was still mystified.

'Don't you know who it is, Kent?' Isobel laughed. 'It's Jack Summers, without his beard!'

Isobel's pale cheeks became, of a sudden, madder-tinged and Shelby's hitherto detached mind began to throw off some of its cobwebs.

'Are you–?' he stopped short suddenly, waiting for the girl to help him.

The red hair glinted in the sun as she nodded. 'Mr Summers – Jack – and I are – going to be married,' she whispered. 'Then I'm going to Sage Junction for the operation–'

'Operation?'

'Didn't Doc Cleary tell you? He's done a fine job, Kent, and both of you together have saved my life. I'll always be eternally grateful.'

'Amen to that,' Jack Summers said huskily.

'The surgeon's already been to see me and has said there's no real danger now, but an operation will put everything right.' She laughed happily. 'It's just a – a sort of formality.'

Shelby came alive at last.

'I'm glad, Isobel, and for you too, Jack,' he said softly. 'There's been enough violence and bloodshed and hatred, yes, and suffering. It's time folk were happy again.'

He came out on to the board-walk feeling strangely alive now. The demons were gone and Charlie Colfax's memory was no longer a haunting ghost but a friendly spirit.

He strolled down the walk and entered Guyler's store as the big man came forward to shake his hand.

'Can settle with you now, Henry,' Kent grinned. 'Thanks to Cal and Charlie and Harry and your boy, we didn't do too badly out of the trail drive.'

'Heard you'd only lost about seventy head, Kent,' Henry Guyler said. 'Not bad, considering.'

There was something strange about Guyler suddenly, Kent thought. His last words had been delivered with a coolness unlike his usual hearty warmth. Now he had excused himself and gone into the rooms at back of the store and Kent wondered what he had said to produce such a sudden effect. He absently toyed with some of the miscellaneous articles scattered across the counter. What had he said? He had mentioned the trail-drive and how the boys had helped…

He heard a slight noise behind him and turned and saw her standing there in the rear doorway and felt suddenly as though all the beauty in nature and the wild living things had merged and coalesced together to form this lovely thing.

She was dressed for travelling and carried a small valise. Gone was the riding outfit. Gone was the ranch- and trail-hand. In their place stood a woman. Infinitely beautiful. Infinitely desirable.

He noted that her cheeks were nearly as pale as those of Isobel Montago and underneath the black-fringed green eyes were dark, bluish smudges.

'Hello, Kent,' she said and her voice was low and controlled. Shelby knew then that he had been dead for the past two and a half weeks and was alive again.

He came towards her and took her arm. 'Where are you going, Donna?'

She gave a shaky, throaty laugh that to Selby, with his newborn awareness, was not quite convincing. 'Where else but to Sage Junction, where I was going before, Kent? There's nothing here in Warpath, or the valley to stop me–'

He took her in his arms, suddenly and crushed her mouth against his.

She resisted at first, but her defences were crumbling and she knew it, and presently she returned his kiss.

'Will that stop you, Donna?' he said after a while.

'What does a kiss mean, Kent?' she countered huskily.

'This one means I want you to be my wife. To share Sugar Loaf with me—'

'What else?'

'It means that I love you, Donna,' he said in a low voice. 'I couldn't come before. I had some unfinished business to attend to. Something to do with a man called Charlie Colfax.'

'It is finished now, Kent? For good and all?'

He nodded and bent to kiss her once more.

This Large Print Book, for people
who cannot read normal print,
is published under the auspices of

THE ULVERSCROFT FOUNDATION

... we hope you have enjoyed this book.
Please think for a moment about those
who have worse eyesight than you ...
and are unable to even read or enjoy
Large Print without great difficulty.

You can help them by sending a
donation, large or small, to:

**The Ulverscroft Foundation,
1, The Green, Bradgate Road,
Anstey, Leicestershire, LE7 7FU,
England.**
or request a copy of our brochure for
more details.

The Foundation will use all donations
to assist those people who are visually
impaired and need special attention
with medical research, diagnosis
and treatment.

Thank you very much for your help.